the snuff syndicate

Published 2012 by Beating Windward Press LLC

For contact information, please visit:
www.BeatingWindward.com

Copyright © Beating Windward Press, 2012

Tipping The Odds: Copyright © C.A. Burns, 2011.
"E": Copyright © Kevin Cockle, 2011.
NSFW: Copyright © Lorne Dixon, 2011.
On the Prowl, Birth of an Idea, Bound By Blood, Scratching The Itch, The Killers' Challenge, Alone in the Night, Work of Art, To The Victor Goes The Spoils, & Giving the Finger: Copyright © Keith Gouveia, 2012.
The Calling: Copyright © Giovanna Lagana, 2011.
Shall We Dance: Copyright © Mark Onspaugh, 2011.
Hackwork: Copyright © Gerald S. Parker, 2011.
First Communion: Copyright © Marsheila Rockwell, 2011.
Snuffingly Yours: Copyright © J. T. Seate, 2011.

All Rights Reserved
Cover Design: Copyright © House of Thuan, 2012
Book Design: Copyright © KP Creative, 2012

First Edition
ISBN: 978-0-9838252-4-1

These are works of fiction. Names, characters, places and incidents are the product of the author's imagination or are used fictitiously. Any resemblance to actual persons, living or dead, business establishments, events, or locales is entirely coincidental.

the snuff syndicate

A Novella by Keith Gouveia

*Interwoven with Stories by
C.A. Burns, Kevin Cockle, Lorne Dixon,
Giovanna Lagana, Mark Onspaugh,
Gerald S. Parker, Marsheila Rockwell, & J. T. Seate*

TABLE

On the Prowl by Keith Gouveia 1

Hackwork by Gerald S. Parker 5

Birth of an Idea by Keith Gouveia 33

Tipping The Odds by C.A. Burns 37

Bound By Blood by Keith Gouveia 57

First Communion by Marsheila Rockwell 65

Scratching The Itch by Keith Gouveia 79

The Calling by Giovanna Lagana 87

The Killers' Challenge by Keith Gouveia 101

"E" by Kevin Cockle 105

Alone in the Night by Keith Gouveia 123

Snuffingly Yours by J. T. Seate 127

Work of Art by Keith Gouveia 139

Shall we Dance by Mark Onspaugh 149

To The Victor Goes The Spoils by Keith Gouveia 161

NSFW by Lorne Dixon 167

Giving the Finger by Keith Gouveia 191

Author Bios 195

<on the prowl>
Keith Gouveia

Peter turned away from the dead body lying in a growing pool of blood and looked upon Mike. The devilish grin on Mike's face sickened him. Peter threw a quick jab to Mike's bicep.

"Hey!" Mike rubbed the spot; his lips pursed and puffed out.

"Why'd you slit her throat? I can't get a good shot."

Mike punched his friend back. "Why'd you make so much noise picking the lock?"

"I didn't!" Peter raised his hand for another hit.

Mike flinched. "She surprised me, that's all. Sorry."

Peter lowered his hand, unable to stay mad at Mike. *Could she have heard the tumblers disengaging or...?* His gaze traveled over her slender frame. Fresh make-up, sleek red dress, and sequined purse told him otherwise.

"You think she was meeting someone?" Mike gave voice to what Peter was thinking.

"She's a total bitch. How could anyone?"

Like Peter, Julie Lynn was a steady patron at the Drink No Evil Cafe, but she lacked courtesy, even common decency, and was continually abusive to the coffee shop baristas. Her badgering and complaining of the sweet girls was border-line bullying, a crime punishable by death.

When Peter saw Julie waltz up and dump her full cup across the counter because her coffee tasted too good to be soy milk, the urge to kill came on stronger than ever.

The day had started out with the razor's edge of an art critic. Followed by Mike's incessant whining about how the shop's monkey décor creeped him out, despite the fact that he could not recall inviting him along. Then the traffic jam in the heart of downtown Orlando. Whether it was Karma or a god he didn't believe in working against him, he didn't know. All Peter wanted was a fine cup of coffee and to enjoy a smile brought on from the whimsical monkeys. The three mystic apes could be seen on the cups, napkins, and sugar dispensers, there were even a few lamps with the monkeys portrayed totem style. Though he had to admit the décor was over the top, there was just something about the collection that tickled his fancy.

Mike shrugged and broke the silence, "With legs like that, I'd tolerate it."

Peter punched him in the arm once more.

"What the hell?"

"That was for stealing the kill."

"Damn…that one hurt."

"*Pft!*"

Looking as if he had just been sent to his room by his mother, Mike stepped away from him, out of arm's reach.

"You can be such a girl," Peter said.

"And you can be a…." Mike stopped short

Peter knew where he was going. "I'm sorry. You're right. You needed it just as much as I did."

"You can have the next one," said Mike. "It won't be so long again."

"If you're right that she had a date, we better hurry up. Someone might come looking."

"What about your picture?"

Peter released a nasal sigh. He bent at the knees and examined the jagged wound, the fear in her final moments still etched on her face and behind her terror-filled eyes. "I'll just have to mentally block out your hack job. Do me a favor."

"Anything," Mike said, looking eager to please.
"Turn her head a little to the left."
"You got it!"

Peter simply shook his head at Mike's eagerness to get his hands dirty, but he supposed it was one of the quirky things about him that made their partnership work. Looking down at their latest victim through the camera lens, he said, "Perfect!"

Mike stepped away, out of the frame, and Peter snapped the shot. Satisfied with the picture, he lowered the camera. "All right," he said, pulling the pliers from his back pocket.

Mike nodded, then dropped to one knee and leaned her head back.

With the pliers in hand, Peter chose an upper incisor and pulled. It popped off like a chunk of cement. He stumbled backward and fell on his ass.

"What happened?" asked Mike with a trace of a smile.

Peter held up his prize and narrowed his eyes upon it. "A cap. Sonuvabitch." He flung the falsehood with the flick of his wrist. "Vain bitch! They better not all be veneers. I can't work with inferior materials."

"There's plenty of others. Try again."

"If I have to settle for a molar, I'm going to be pissed," Peter said as he got back on his feet.

He positioned himself again; this time bracing his foot on the floor and gripped the other upper incisor with just the right amount of force so as not to slip off or crush the tooth. It was a balance he had learned over the years with practice. *Excellent,* he thought, *resistance*. Peter adjusted his footing and worked it back and forth. With a splintering crackle, the tooth was wrenched free. The force sent him backward, but this time he remained upright.

Before he had a chance to marvel over his prize, Mike growled, "My turn." And held up his pruning shears.

<Hackwork>
Gerald S. Parker

Had the Monet drifted askew? Oliver fussed with the print until it hung just so. Then he repositioned the two amateur pastels on either side of it to balance the composition. Little room remained on the wall behind the register, but the design cried out for one more work. After a moment's debate he selected one of his own, a small watercolor of the park at sunset.

He had killed his seventh model there, right at the foot of the tree. When he looked up, his fingers still warm from the young man's skin, he'd been struck by the view from that angle, the natural symmetries of the park juxtaposed against the stark artificial regimentation of the city beyond. How would it look at sunset? He'd gone back a few days later, once the swarms of detectives and reporters were gone, and stepped around the tattered crime scene tape to make pastel sketches as the sun went down.

He pinned it to the wall, stepped around the counter, studied the final effect, and finally nodded. Yes, that would work. Not that his customers would notice anything except for pretty colors but it still might brighten their day.

Mrs. Blake tottered up to the register, this month's batch of bodice-rippers and the morning paper in her basket. "Good morning, Mr. Hewitt." She peered beyond his head. "Oh, there's a new one."

"It's the park."

"Yes, I think I know the place. There's that big old oak.

The colors are just perfect. I almost feel like I'm there."

"Thank you. I tried so hard to make the colors vibrant, but water's so difficult to work with. I may have to take a class in oils."

"One of yours?"

He nodded, pleased. "It's nothing spectacular."

"I think it's lovely, Mr. Hewitt. You have a real talent."

"Mrs. Blake, you're a shameless flatterer. This is dabbling. It's nowhere near good enough to be called art."

"You're too modest."

"And you're too kind." He rang up the novels one by one, eyes fastidiously averted from the lurid covers. He considered Mrs. Blake a good customer, in spite of her atrocious taste in reading material. "Have you been down to Milan's yet? You've just got to try the new almond coffee."

"Bull." She waggled her finger at him. "You're trying to set me up with that Mr. Prentiss."

"I wouldn't dream of playing games with you." Oliver smiled and placed the books and newspaper back in her basket, along with the receipt. "I just feel a lovely lady such as yourself shouldn't go about town unescorted. Especially not these days."

"You're telling me. Did you see this morning's paper?"

She unfolded her own copy for his edification. "Royston Ripper Strikes Again" blared back at him in stark forty-eight-point type.

"I've seen it." He touched the paper gingerly, and made a show of skimming the first few paragraphs for politeness's sake. Headlines again. How gauche. He folded the paper, front page and its offensive banner primly tucked away, and returned it to Mrs. Blake. "I try not to read those stories. They're too disturbing."

"It's getting so it's not safe to walk the streets in broad daylight anymore. I feel like I ought to hire a bodyguard."

"Mr. Prentiss has a cane."

"Mr. Prentiss is a wimp. I need a nice young hunk. Somebody who could give a little old lady some real protection."

"With an attitude like that, Mrs. Blake, you will never be old." Smiling, Oliver walked her to the door and held it for her while she hobbled outside. "Enjoy your day."

His smile disappeared the moment she left. He marched back to the counter without favoring the newspaper rack with so much as a glance. Another dead girl found in an alley, or on the street or some such. Grab a girl at random and hack her to bits. How drearily tiresome.

Oliver shook his head. The city had always been his own personal canvas. He'd had it all arranged just so. Then this "Royston Ripper" appeared. Wasn't it just like the Visigoths to come along and threaten everything?

The man had no flair whatsoever. No variation in the pattern. No creativity, no artistry at all. These people never grew, never improved, never learned. Just another talentless hack.

Caution advised Oliver to quell his own urges until this monster was caught. But what was an artist to do when inspiration struck? Sip a glass of cold water and have a nice lie-down until the impulse passed? Where would the world be if Picasso and Gauguin had felt that way? Still hurtling down the road to Hell, no doubt, but probably at an even brisker pace.

The musings stirred him, and he dug a Gauguin print out of a drawer and added it to the display. His own effort now looked shoddy in comparison, but he left the watercolor up regardless. Perhaps the spirit of the master would shine upon him, and he would discover a new way to see. He returned to his duties with a cheerier heart.

Art, in Oliver Hewitt's philosophy, marked man's separation from lower forms of life. The ability to both create and appreciate ambitious flights of fancy set humankind above the beasts and into the realms of the gods. Whether it was painting, music, literature, or an exquisitely prepared meal with the perfect wine, art in all its many forms was infinitely precious to him.

He tried to favor the classics when stocking the shelves at his modest shop on the square. He couldn't always succeed. Here in the mundane world, bills had to be paid and even gross appetites satisfied. This meant carrying inventory that would sell: paperback romances, the latest spew by some flavor-of-the-month best-selling author, "autobiographies" by celebrities who had been through drug rehab and the sorry groupies who had slept with them. Oliver had positioned these racks near the wall, in plain sight of his customers but hidden from his own offended eyes by the tall discount shelves near the counter. He might have to sell such trash to stay in business, but he wasn't about to have it rubbed in his face day after day.

"Hackwork," he called it, though never to the customers, who gobbled it down like greasy chips. The coarsening of America, Oliver would think, and sadly shake his head.

He fought it off in little ways, with displays of art prints and calendars at the register, discounted coffee table books on fine art, and brochures advertising local writers' workshops and readers' groups. Then there was the gallery on the wall behind the register, comprised of his own and customers' efforts, drawings, sketches and watercolor studies, posted optimistically close to the works of acknowledged masters, as if proximity might somehow impart genius.

Only Oliver's conventional works went up on the wall in the bookstore. At home, tucked away in a leather portfolio at the back of his closet, were the records of his true calling, his real art.

Pencil, charcoal, paint, pastel: all too flat, too lacking in dimension. None of these would ever truly inspire him. He tried sculpture, but found wood and marble cold beneath his hands. Clay came closest; it could be warmed, could be shaped to match the living visions in his mind. But even clay proved insufficient in the end.

He discovered his métier when he was fifteen, when his father came after him with the belt one time too many. Ben Hewitt never appreciated the son Fate had sent him—too small, far too sensitive, as thin and pallid as his wispy blond hair, no good at hunting or sports. *What kind of pansy boy are you?* his father always snarled, usually to the accompaniment of a blow, while Mother wrung her hands and stood by, helpless against this brute she'd married.

So Oliver doused his beer with drain cleaner. Now let Daddy see what kind of boy he was.

Eventually his sire's writhing and retching grew tiresome, so Oliver put an end to it with a well-aimed clout from a chunk of wood retrieved from the pile outside. As the body lay cooling on the kitchen floor, young Oliver, prompted by a sudden vision, straightened it from its final cramped rictus, posed it with the wooden club in its hand, and used a charcoal stick to sketch in a heavy brow and a ragged beard. *The Fall of Neanderthal Man.* He looked so much more interesting that way.

They buried him in the woodlot out back and told the police Hewett the Elder had run off with some townie tramp. No one questioned them. Everybody knew Ben Hewett's tastes. No one realized young Oliver's tastes had just taken a life-altering turn.

Inspiration had bloomed in Oliver's soul.

After that, he experimented with frogs netted from a nearby pond, then with squirrels and finally stray dogs and cats lured to the porch with pungent garbage. He studied taxidermy, but abandoned it. A lasting record wasn't what he wanted. He wanted to make a brief but telling statement, like a swift, pure stab through the heart. Dead flesh worked best for this. Dying flesh even better.

In the fifteen years since he'd turned Ben Hewitt from paternal corpse into artistic creation, Oliver had labored hard to perfect his skills. It prodded him into watercolors; charcoal couldn't capture the nuances of color and shade in cooling flesh.

His second human model was an arrogant young snot he encountered during his freshman year at college. Intelligent, athletic, popular with women, proud of his good looks. He'd chosen Oliver as the butt of his painful practical jokes. Oliver chose poison, so as not to ruin the model's appearance. He arranged the body carefully on a flat slab of rock by a lake off campus: the perfect Narcissus, dead eyes staring eternally at his own reflection.

Back in his dorm room, still flush with excitement, Oliver sketched the scene from memory. It turned out better than he expected. In that moment his career as an artist was set.

His portfolio comprised a journal of seven opuses, each more ambitious than the last. The critics—he counted law enforcement foremost among them—didn't understand what he was trying to say. He wondered if anyone did, if aesthetic sensibilities still existed in this crude and coarsened world.

And now this slipshod amateur had moved in on his palette, feeding the public's lust for blood instead of nurturing their imagination. Perhaps it was time to select a new model, create a new canvas, show people the marked difference between hackwork and true art.

He poured through several books of masters' works for inspiration, but nothing came. He was not surprised, or disappointed. Art could not be forced. Trust in your talent, he told himself. It had never let him down.

Whenever Oliver suffered creative block, he would visit the city park, three acres of woods, greens, and jogging paths crammed into an urban setting. A brisk two-block walk from the bookstore brought him to his favorite bench, which afforded him a clear view of the most frequented path. Here he could eat lunch while studying the potential models who jogged, power walked, rollerbladed or strolled past him, oblivious to their possible roles in artistic history. He brought his sketchpad with him, to capture fleeting ideas.

Today was perfect for renewing one's artistic soul: sky by early June, temperatures held over from spring. On days like these people were driven to shed their clothes like layers of skin, and bare for him the many possibilities.

Two young, up-and-coming executives strode rapidly past, ties loosened and jackets slung over shoulders, arguing over some sporting event. No inspiration there. He let them pass. His eye was drawn to a woman with two little girls, a toddler in a flowered dress and an infant in a stroller. He had never worked with children, and had no intention of doing so. Children's bright, quicksilver lives were already masterpieces his feeble efforts could not improve upon. He smiled at the woman and waved to the little girl, who giggled and waved back.

A pair of teen lovers drifted over the grass, utterly lost in each other. Oliver gazed after them thoughtfully, but in the end bent his head to nibble at his sandwich. He'd created that tableau already, a stunning Pyramis and Thisbe on the steps of the public library. He'd draped a woman's scarf and smeared the girl's blood on one of the building's stone lions to complete the allusion. Of course the critics didn't get it. "A sick joke," one reviewer had labeled it. That hadn't stopped the papers from running the story on page one. Oliver sniffed at the memory. Artistic vision twisted into sensationalism. What else could one expect of the media?

He was reaching for his carton of iced tea when a flash of electric blue caught his attention. A jogger went sailing—practically floating—up the path across the park. He recognized her by her hair, a savage shade of red, today half-tamed and firmly bound in a bouncy ponytail. He saw her often; she jogged in the park three times a week. But that had been in sweat suits, or jackets and jeans. Today she'd left her bulky garments behind, in favor of a college T-shirt and those painfully blue jogging shorts. It changed her entire look, her whole potential.

Oliver's widening eyes tracked her progress. She was built like a deer: willowy and golden-skinned, long-limbed, graceful and fleet. Even that wondrous hair called to mind a roe's pelt. He stared, hypnotized by the muscular pumping of her legs as she made her circuit of the park.

Diana.

He felt the familiar punch of inspiration, hot and nearly crippling in its ethereal sweetness. Diana, goddess of the hunt. His mind's eye dressed her in a short-skirted tunic and placed a bow in her hands. The image sang through him with the force of an orgasm. Diana. His next creation.

"Some looker, huh?"

Startled from his trance, Oliver glanced around. A man stood beside his bench, one hand resting lightly on its back. He was maybe in his early thirties, with an arrogant profile and black hair that curled like a ram's fleece. He leered after the jogger. "They broke the mold after they poured those legs."

"I couldn't imagine," Oliver said stiffly. Such urges never bothered him when he was creating. That wasn't what models were for.

He dismissed the man from his thoughts and turned them back to the jogger. She swung around a curve in the path and left the park. The focus of his lusting gone, the ram's-haired man moved on. So did Oliver. There was so much to do. He gathered up the remains of his lunch and hurried back to the bookstore.

Oliver spent the evening reacquainting himself with myths and depictions of the goddess Diana. He studied her image in painting and sculpture, skimmed his many tomes on mythology, one hand flipping pages, the other feverishly sketching. He needed to uncover the commonalities and distill them through his perceptions to fashion his own unique interpretation. No copies or retreads for Oliver Hewitt; he created only originals.

Props. He would need a bow. A child's toy would do, easily and anonymously purchased at any department store. Diana was often depicted with a deer. The petting zoo over in Lakewood had a small herd, but also high fences. He might have to make do with a lawn ornament, tacky though they looked. A simple linen sheet would form her tunic. Perhaps a wreath of cypress leaves for her hair.

Setting was harder. He delved into his copious memories of the park. As her brother Apollo was god of the sun, so Diana was identified with the moon. A clearing, then, someplace open to the sky and kissed by moonlight. He would need to walk the park at night, get a feel for its moods, find exactly the perfect background to best display his work.

He added her face to his drawing, sketched from memory as expertly as if she stood before him. He included a cocoa-eyed doe, and surrounded both with a nimbus of moonlight. He held it up to admire it. Not yet perfect; this was only a draft. The reality would be perfect. "Diana," he murmured. "Beautiful. Immortal. They'll remember you for decades to come."

A few more sketches, a little more planning, a couple of minor details. Then he could begin work on his creation. Oliver went to bed a happy man.

For the next three days Oliver ate his lunch in the park, hoping to glimpse his new model. She rewarded him twice. He was able to capture her likeness in motion, adding the details—the bow, the moon, the deer—that brought his goddess to life.

The ram's-haired man showed up too, idling on a bench, chugging a soda. He didn't speak to Oliver, and Oliver pointedly ignored him.

He strolled the park by night, and finally found the perfect setting: a little clearing, ringed by trees, spotlighted by the rising moon. Oliver studied the gibbous moon critically. No, that wouldn't do. It must be a full moon. He would have to wait at least a week. He went home to refine his sketches. Everything needed to be exactly right.

Then it all went disastrously wrong.

He was sitting on his bench, with his sandwich and carton of tea, when Diana appeared—with a partner. She jogged in tandem with the ram's-haired man. They glided by in perfect step, past Oliver's bench. Shocked, he dropped his pencil. His stare followed them around the bend in the path and out of sight.

Of course his models had families, friends and mundane lives. He'd worked around such hindrances before. But this? Diana—his masterpiece—consorting with that uncouth brute? Hadn't she any sense of taste?

He fumbled for his pencil, found it, snatched it up. It snapped between his fingers.

The next day, and the following two, she ran with her new lover. Oliver filled his pad with vicious sketches of the man dying in myriad violent ways. He crafted two perfect portraits of Ram's Hair, one full on, one profile. Perhaps the Muse would be kind and inspire a second work, one in which Diana's swain could star. But no such comfort came. They jogged around the park, fixated on each other, unaware he watched them through narrowed, seething eyes.

He followed them. Hunted them, as the goddess of the chase pursued wild game. They would arrive separately, do their run, have coffee at the little sidewalk café across the street. His mouth moved with words that brought smiles and laughter to her perfect lips. His hand stole out to cover hers. Oliver ground his teeth.

He stalked the ram's-haired man, trailed him back to his lair: a squalid apartment house, perfect for transients. His worst assumptions were confirmed. This creature wasn't fit to consort with his Diana. His filth would only sully her. He must act quickly, and create his work while his model still bore the glow of purity.

The next afternoon, a torrential downpour kept everyone out of the park. Oliver was back on his bench the following day. His most heartfelt desire was granted: Diana jogged alone. He slipped away to his car before she completed her run, then tailed her back to her apartment. He watched her enter the building, noted the position and floor of the window she flung open, scribbled the address.

He had his props: a toy bow, linen for the tunic, a deer hide and horns he'd found at a sports shop. In the end he couldn't bring himself to use a kitschy lawn ornament; the deer hide, fastened with the horns, would serve both as Diana's cloak and a symbolic representation of her signature animal. He had his setting, the clearing in the park. The moonbeams would slip like furtive lovers through the leaves, and paint her skin with ivory and turn her hair to flame. He had his bottle of chloroform, and his ropes and duct tape. She would not be alarmed when he approached her. He was as much a fixture in the park as the benches or the trees. The familiarity would get him close enough to clamp the rag over her nostrils. He would have to use poison again. There must be no wounds or bruises to mar the impact of her beauty.

Oliver shivered in anticipation. He was ready to create.

He decided on Saturday night, Sunday morning at the latest. Saturday was the first night of the full moon. By Sunday night, if fortune favored him, his work would be on display for all to see, and for those few with the proper artist's spirit to appreciate.

For inspiration he hung one of his sketches on the board behind the counter: Diana, racing through the woods in the moonlight with her signature deer beside her, bow in hand, lips parted and eyes alive with the thrill of the hunt. Her face was that of the jogger in the park. He felt a fleeting twinge of regret that he hadn't learned his model's name. Ah well, after Sunday night, she would forever be Diana.

At eight o'clock Oliver locked the store for the night and made one last dry run. He cruised his car by her apartment house. No light behind her curtains. Off on a date with her lover, no doubt. Oliver shrugged it off. The night was still newborn. He drove on to the park.

Few people went abroad in the park after sunset, even on a weekend. None paid attention to Oliver, and he paid little to them. He made his way to his clearing, and consulted his watch while he critically observed the fall of light from the newly-risen moon. Too early; the rays were still too harsh. Later, then, maybe around eleven, when the moon had gained some height and its light had mellowed. Then it would be fit to shine upon a goddess.

He was halfway back to his car when he heard the scream.

Normally Oliver didn't embroil himself in others' affairs. But the high, piercing note, and the man's hoarse shout that followed, prompted him to change his course and hustle up the slope in their direction. His loafers found the jogging path. Further down its line he spied the couple, standing over a lump on the ground. The girl had stopped screaming, but even with the dark and distance Oliver could see her shaking, like a mass of leaves in an unexpected storm. She couldn't have been more than twenty, the boy with his arms clamped around her shoulders little older. He panted "Jesus" over and over.

The girl gave a little gasping half-scream when Oliver trotted up. The boy spat "Jesus!" one more time, and backed himself and his girlfriend away from the path and what lay beside it.

Oliver didn't bother to question them. He could see for himself the out-flung leg, still clad in its Nike, that jutted from the weeds onto the path. Moonlight glinted on dark liquid in the grass, already congealed like corrupted dew.

Oliver grimaced. Slash and go. The Visigoth once again at work. More from curiosity than any real concern, he stepped forward to see who had fallen to the Royston Ripper this time.

His eyes found skin moon-washed to ivory, auburn hair set aflame—not vibrant, as he had imagined her, but dulled by the effrontery of murder. No goddess now, his Diana lay in the dirt with her throat and stomach torn open and her limbs splayed like a broken puppet's. Butchered like a cow and left to rot.

Tears started to Oliver's eyes—for the utter waste of it, the tragic loss to art. His cry was no scream, but a full-throated roar. He fell beside the body, his hands tangling in her hair. She would inspire no one now. All her glory, lost forever.

"Jesus, man," the boy said, as if from an eternity away. "Did you know her?"

"Yes." Though no one else would ever see now what she could have been. He had been robbed, the world of art cheated, because of some talentless hack. He forced himself to look away, up at the boy and his shivering lover, both staring back at him with huge saucer eyes. "I'll stay with her," he told them. "Go get help."

The couple stumbled off, picking up speed as they ran. Oliver sat beside the body, smoothing her fiery hair.

His eyes burned with tears, his heart with loss, his soul with inspiration thwarted. "This will not go unpunished," he whispered to her. "This atrocity will be avenged. I promise you."

The man who brought Oliver the mug of black coffee introduced himself as Detective Sam McCaffrey. Oliver recoiled from the mug, and politely declined. He'd endured far too much police station coffee over the last two hours. Detective McCaffrey shrugged and gulped the brew himself. He had the build and dark looks of an ancient warrior, a Biblical hero with a five o'clock shadow and a pistol strapped to his hip. A brief image of the man shattering the pillars of a Philistine temple flitted across Oliver's mind. He tucked it away. Another time. "How can I help you, Detective?"

McCaffrey squinted tight and weary eyes. "You were with those kids when they found the body?"

"Not exactly. I've already given my statement to –"

"I like to hear things straight from the source. In your own words, Mr. Hewitt."

So Oliver recounted again his movements of the evening, or such of them as were relevant. An evening drive, a casual stroll around the park in the moonlight, the scream, the grisly discovery. Toward the end, his throat closed on him. His outrage made it difficult to speak.

"You say you knew the victim?"

"Yes. No. That's a bit misleading. I didn't know her personally. I never even knew her name. I often saw her jogging in the park." His goddess, taken from him. Taken from the world. "Such a tragedy. Such a terrible waste."

"Yeah." McCaffrey downed the rest of the coffee. Oliver wondered if he even tasted it anymore. Or could taste anything after drinking it. "Crap. No trouble at all for years, then two serial killers decide to set up shop in the city at the same time. How did we ever get so lucky?" He stretched his mouth, but it wasn't a smile. "At least we can rule out Mike on this one."

"I beg your pardon?"

"Michelangelo, the artist killer. You don't follow the papers?" Oliver shook his head, feigning ignorance. McCaffrey grunted. "Mike's been around longer. Likes to poison his victims, then arrange them in little scenes, usually out of classical mythology. He did this one on the library steps. Guy and a girl and a lion. Pyramus and what's her name, Frisbee."

"Thisbe," Oliver corrected.

"Thisbe. Right." McCaffrey slanted a look at him. "You know the story?"

"I do own a bookstore, detective." He eyed the man with new respect. "I'm surprised you recognized it. One doesn't expect a cop to—I mean—oh dear. I've put my foot in it up to the ankle, haven't I?"

"S'okay." McCaffrey grinned, this time all the way up to his tight eyes. "I used to love those old movies with the Greek mythology in 'em. Or the Sinbad pictures. Those Ray Harryhausen stop-motion monsters, y'know?"

"I'm sorry, I can't recall having seen one." Oliver's enthusiasm chilled. So much for cops and high art. "So if it isn't…Mike…you suspect the other one?"

"The Royston Ripper?" He grimaced over the name. "Yeah, it looks like his MO. Single girl between nineteen and thirty, beats her up and slits her throat. Then he gets creative."

Creative. Oliver seethed. Creative! As if an untutored brute like the Ripper could even comprehend the meaning of the word. He had to be stopped. "How soon will you be making an arrest?"

"How soon? Geez. I'd like to have the bastard right in front of me right now. Sorry, Mr. Hewitt. I can't say. This Ripper's a sly one. This is his fifth time at bat, and we still don't have a clue. I was hoping maybe you or those two kids had seen something. Anything at all would be a help."

"I'm sorry. It was all over long before I got there. What about her boyfriend? Have you spoken to him yet?"

"Boyfriend?"

"Yes. Tall young fellow, dark curly hair. They just started jogging together over the last week. She'd always jogged alone before. I just assumed—"

"A boyfriend." McCaffrey rubbed his stubble. "Yeah, that would be a help. I don't suppose you know where to find him."

"You mean he hasn't been here? But I thought—"

Oliver stopped himself. Quite a crowd had gathered by the time the ambulance arrived, drawn by the sirens and the screams. He was certain he'd spotted the ram's-haired man slouching about at its edges. He'd swung close to the ambulance more than once. Surely close enough to recognize his lover's unmistakable hair, if not her face. How odd that he hadn't pressed forward, asked the usual set of curious questions, as everyone else had been doing.

Unless, perhaps, he hadn't needed answers.

"You thought?" McCaffrey prompted.

"I thought I saw him at the scene. I must have been mistaken." But not about this, or the hideous suspicion that suddenly bloomed in his mind.

"A boyfriend," McCaffrey repeated. "Well, I'll take anything I can get. He could at least help us pin down her last movements. Can you give us a description?"

"I can do better," Oliver said. "Do you have a pencil and paper?"

Within the hour Oliver supplied McCaffrey with a detailed portrait of Ram's-hair. He had little trouble calling up the man's face; he'd sketched it often enough. In the margins he scribbled his guesses as to Ram's-hair's height, age and weight. The man's address he kept to himself, lest the police wonder how he knew it. This McCaffrey was altogether too keen a blade.

Besides, Oliver had his own theories that required disproving. Or proving.

McCaffrey nodded over the drawing. "Not bad. I mean it. This is really good. You an artist?"

"Oh, no. This is just a hobby of mine. My talent was never the equal of my aspirations."

"Yeah, ain't that always the way. I'll get this into circulation, see if we can turn him up. Thanks, Mr. Hewitt." He handed Oliver a card. "You think of anything else, any little thing at all, you call me. I want this bastard off the streets."

Oliver stood and shook hands with McCaffrey. "You and me both, Detective."

No sandwich in the park today. Oliver spent his lunch hour in the library at a computer terminal, with the morning paper beside him. The headlines trumpeted the news of the Ripper's latest attack. Ancillary stories touted the fear of the local citizenry, the outrage of women's groups, an FBI profiler's take on the Ripper's motives, and assurances from the police department that they were "following up on all available leads." Oliver sniffed. One could take any one of the four previous stories, change a few names and a little phraseology, and come up with today's front page.

He poured over those previous four stories. The Ripper had been inflicting his atrocious propensities on the public for about seven months now. He had a preference for attractive single women in their twenties. He tended to kill on a Friday or Saturday. The bodies were always found quickly, usually within twelve hours of the act. He left them where they would be easily found, as if he were taunting the police.

Oliver scowled at the screen. The Ripper was a simple

butcher, bereft of imagination. Tediously consistent. He followed well-worn patterns in his selection and dispatching of victims. Perhaps also in how he approached them.

Snapshots of four dead women smiled up at him from the computer screen. He had folded the paper so he wouldn't have to look at the fifth, the face of his Diana. Had the other four girls also met a new lover, shortly before their deaths? A tall man in his thirties, perhaps, with smirking eyes and tight curly hair? Murder victims, it was said, often knew their killer.

Along with the victims' names he found lists of relatives. He pulled out a small notebook and filled page after page with meticulous printing. At the circulation desk he asked for a telephone book.

Oliver spent the next three days tracking down survivors. He showed them his two views of Ram's-hair. It's about the murder, he told them. I'm working with the police. He was greeted, more often than not, with relief. Someone besides themselves was taking an interest in their loved one's death. Somebody else wanted justice.

One family—a mother and a brother—said their lost one had mentioned meeting a man scant days before the attack. They hadn't met him. There hadn't been time. The mother burst into tears. The brother sent him down the street to visit with the victim's cousin. The girls had been close as sisters. The cousin nodded vigorously over Oliver's drawings. The hair had been blond, she told him, but still tightly curled as a fleece, and she recognized the arrogant jut of his nose. "Yeah, that's him," she said. "Jimmy something. We all went out for coffee once. Rae said he was the greatest guy on Earth. He was nice, especially after, well, you know. He sent flowers and everything."

"I'm sure he did," Oliver said. "Thank you. You've been most helpful."

"I've found him," he told the drawing of Diana, still pinned to the board behind the register.

He smiled to his customers, chatted with them, rang up their purchases, went through the motions of running the store while he considered his next move.

All was in readiness. He knew the butcher's name and where he laired. The cousin had given him proof. A quick stop on his way to the bookstore this morning had gained him the last of the items he needed. He had known almost from the first the form Diana's retribution must take.

"Tonight," he told the Diana on the wall. "Tonight there will be justice."

The front door swung open, jangling the bell. Startled, Oliver looked up. "Oh, Detective McCaffrey." He leaned across the counter. "Has there been any progress in the case?"

"Not yet." McCaffrey paused to glance around the store. "Nice place. You've got it all here, don't you?" His glance wandered toward the paperback shelves. "Any Elmore Leonard?"

Oliver hid his wince. "Perhaps next week."

McCaffrey nodded and ambled up to the register. "We've been showing that picture around. You were right, he may have had something to do with her. People recognized him right off. May I say, Mr. Hewitt, you've got a helluvan eye."

"Thank you."

"Don't thank me yet." McCaffrey leaned on the counter, so that his jacket fell open and his pistol showed. His eyes were thin and hard. "We've been talking to the families of the other victims, trying to pin down a pattern. Imagine our surprise when we found out some other guy'd already been around. Slender fellah, average height, kind'a thin blond hair. Showing the same drawing we've got and asking a lot of questions." He lifted his stern glare from Oliver's eyes to his wispy cornsilk hair. "Anybody you know?"

"I only wanted to help."

"Well, don't. That stuff may work on TV, but in real life we don't appreciate it. We've got leads. We may be close to catching the guy. You can help us most by staying the hell out of it."

"Of course, Detective. I'm sorry. I hope I haven't jeopardized your investigation."

"Not this time. Just confused a lot of people and pissed off a lot of tired cops. But that sketch of yours is the first break we've had in seven months. That's the only reason I'm not running you in, and I won't if you keep your nose out of police business from here on in. We have a deal?"

Oliver nodded, with just the right amount of contrition. McCaffrey stepped back, and his gaze darted beyond Oliver's head to the "gallery." "Holy—did you do that?"

"Which?"

"Diana. That drawing, next to that painting of the park."

"Diana?" He swallowed hard, and chose his next words carefully. "Yes, that one's mine. So is the park painting. The others were done by customers. I like to encourage local artists."

McCaffrey stepped up for a closer squint. "You told me you didn't know her. That is her, isn't it? The Ripper's last victim?"

"Yes, it is. But I didn't know her, not by name. I used to see her in the park, as I told you. She reminded me of the goddess, so I—"

"She never posed for you? You did that from memory?"

"I did a few rough sketches while she jogged. I drew that after she was…well. Consider it a tribute, if you will."

"From memory." McCaffrey whistled. "Helluvan eye. You remember what I told you. No more detective work." He gave the drawing one last marveling stare and strolled out.

Oliver ducked into the back of the shop and straightened books until his hands relaxed and his breathing grew even again. Too close. That McCaffrey was sharp, for a critic.

Not that it mattered. All he needed was tonight. One must never trifle with art.

Oliver arrived at the butcher's building shortly after dark. Five rusty mailboxes had been fastened in an uneven row beside the front door. Three of the five tenants had considerately taped their names to their boxes, just below the apartment number. Not a J., James, Jim or Jimmy in the lot. That narrowed the field down to two. He got out a spiral notepad, straightened his tie, and proceeded to door number one.

The frowzy blonde woman who answered his knock assured him no James, Jim, or Jimmy lived there, but she could be a Jimmy for him if that's what revved his motor. Oliver thanked her politely, apologized for the intrusion, and moved on to door number two.

Success. The man with the ram-curl hair answered on the third knock. He peered at Oliver with the squinty expression of a man who knows a face, but can't recall from where. "Yeah?"

"Good evening," Oliver said. "I'm conducting a survey for the housing authority, and I was hoping I could ask—"

"At this time of night?"

"I apologize for the hour. It's a big city, and we're horribly understaffed. May I come in, Mr.—?"

"Yeah, okay." Ram's-hair slouched aside, and Oliver stepped within.

He had his script prepared: how long have you lived here; how many rooms; is the landlord quick with repairs; is there a smoke alarm and/or a fire extinguisher; have you been troubled by any pests, e.g., roaches or rats. He scribbled randomly on his pad, barely hearing the man's grunted replies. He was too busy scanning the apartment, looking for clues to a murder. Perhaps he had let his animosity run away with him. The ram's-haired man could be innocent; this could all be a mistake. Before he proceeded with Diana's vengeance, he had to be absolutely sure, or else the work of art would be tainted.

The apartment consisted of one large room, divided only by species of furniture into a living room and bedroom, with a tiny kitchen and an even tinier bath. A couch with frayed cushions marked the living room/bedroom demarcation line. The "bedroom" boasted a lumpy cot and a shabby bureau. A TV sat on a nicked coffee table in a corner. On the flickering, snowy screen a sculpted news anchor declared with detached sincerity war's possible outbreak in the Middle East.

"Hey, waitaminnit. I know you." The man took an aggressive step forward. "You're that guy hangs out in the park. You work for the city?"

"I'm volunteering." Oliver drifted toward the bedroom. "We've had reports of safety violations. Have you ever had any problems with—"

He stopped, and coughed to cover his excitement. His shift in position had brought to his eye a glitter of gold from the bureau. In the harsh light of the naked ceiling bulb he could now see it clearly. Much more clearly than in the black-and-white photo of the Ripper's third victim, when that same trim golden locket had graced a young girl's throat. Before it was gashed open, of course.

"Problems with what?" Ram's-hair demanded.

Oliver turned. Their eyes met. In that instant they recognized each other for what they were. The man's expression didn't change, but he shifted his weight, like a snake rearing up. "Nothing," Oliver said. "I believe I have all I need."

"Goody for you. Glad I could help."

"There is one more thing. Why did you kill all those girls?"

The man with the ram's hair didn't start, or sputter indignant protests. Instead he smiled. "Because I wanted to," he said, and lunged.

This Oliver had expected, and for this he'd come prepared. He was no stranger to physical conflict. His models often struggled. Instead of meeting Ram-hair's charge, he simply stepped aside. No imagination, indeed. It was easy enough to trip him up, send him crashing into his bed. Ram's-hair recovered quickly, but not fast enough to avoid the hypodermic Oliver plunged into his thigh. After that, it was simply a matter of avoiding his clumsy attacks until the drug made him woozy. A blow with the blackjack he'd brought along finished things up quickly.

Heaving the man onto the bed wasn't easy; he was heavier than he looked, and dead weight besides. But the hardest part was over. Oliver tucked the blackjack and hypo away and listened. Ten minutes passed, then fifteen. No one pounded on the wall, or came to the door shouting questions. Quite incurious neighbors this artless butcher had. Incurious, or prudent. Either way, no one was about to come to his defense.

All was in readiness, then. Oliver checked his victim's slow, shallow breathing, then slipped outside to the trunk of his car, to set the final stage.

"Wake up." Oliver slapped the man's face, a gentle tap at first, then harder. "Wake up, beast."

The man moaned. His eyelids fluttered. Oliver stepped away from the bed and watched his slow return to awareness, watched the barbarian's slack face harden into incredulity as he gradually discovered the pose Oliver had positioned him in. His models usually never saw this stage of the creation. Did he appreciate it? Or even recognize its significance? Most likely not.

Oliver paused to admire his handiwork. The man lay spread-eagled on the bed, wrapped in the deerskin and bound to the headboard and frame by lengths of stout rope.

Duct tape splayed his fingers and toes, which Oliver had smeared with black shoe polish to simulate cloven hooves. The antlers he had duct-taped to the man's head, so that they seemed to sprout from his curly hair. They rattled against the headboard with each desperate jerk Ram's-hair made against his bonds. The duct tape across his mouth muffled his words into the grunts of a brute.

"I've been poking around," Oliver said. "I found your collection of newspaper clippings. And your little trophies." All of which he had neatly stacked on the bureau for the police to find. "Those clippings go back a long way. You've been at this for a while. Haven't you, you uncultured savage?"

The man lunged against the ropes. His eyes burned at Oliver. An animal's eyes. Still a predatory animal, but that was about to change. "You've no idea what this is about, do you? I didn't think you would. It's about a woman. A goddess. You ran with her in the park. Do you remember her?"

Ram's-hair shook his head. The antlers clacked like castanets. "Forgotten already," Oliver said. "How typical. She was your last victim. Your very last victim."

Ah. Now it was starting to sink in. He saw what he wanted in the man's eyes: the slow realization, the beginnings of fear. Animal fear. Prey fear. "She was my Diana," Oliver said. "I would have elevated her to art. I would have made her immortal. You made her meat."

The man stared, then shook. Little muffled squeaks leaked out from behind the duct tape. He was laughing. Oliver scowled down at him, and the laughter hissed away. "So you think it's funny. Of course you would. You're just a common hack. No appreciation of art. Well, we've got a little time." Oliver leaned his hip against the bureau. "Let me tell you a story. About a young man, and a goddess.

"His name was Actaeon, and he was a handsome youth. Perhaps with hair like yours. He was hunting in the woods one day when he chanced across a forest pool, and discovered the goddess Diana."

He looked down into the man's twisted, sweaty features. No comprehension. Ah well. "Diana was a virginal goddess, the goddess of the hunt," he explained. "She'd gone to the pool to bathe. Actaeon surprised her in her nakedness. He violated her modesty." He brushed one finger down the stiff deer hide that covered the bound man's body. "As punishment, the insulted goddess turned him into a stag."

The man thrashed, causing Oliver to jerk his hand away. One of the antlers drooped askew. Oliver straightened it. "Actaeon ran, but he was a deer now. His hounds picked up his scent and gave chase."

He reached into his bag and brought out his last prop, the one he had purchased this morning. Sure, the clerk at the sporting goods store had assured him, 'That knife'll skin a buck. No sweat.'

Oliver straightened. His face was terrible in the naked light of the bulb. "The pack ran Actaeon down. He was torn to pieces by his own dogs."

At last, realization caught up with Ram's-hair. He shrieked behind the tape. His eyes were a deer's eyes, panicked and wild. The perfect moment of creation. Oliver moved in.

Oliver was surprised, but not alarmed, when he answered the sound of the bookstore bell and found McCaffrey standing by the counter. "Detective McCaffrey. How can I help you?"

McCaffrey was thumbing through the magazines on the display rack Oliver kept by the register. Oliver noticed he was out of People again. That one always sold out first, that and the tabloids. For the life of him, he couldn't figure why. "Still no Elmore Leonard?" McCaffrey asked him.

"Sorry."

McCaffrey grunted and glanced out the window. There was a police cruiser parked at the curb, with two uniformed cops lounging against it, sipping coffee. "Just thought I'd stop in, see if you'd heard the news."

"I'm sorry, I've been busy this morning, I haven't had the chance. You found the boyfriend?"

"Oh yeah, we found him. Along with a little stack of evidence that may just prove he was the Royston Ripper." McCaffrey paused for dramatic effect. "He'd been murdered."

Oliver put on his well-rehearsed expression of shock. "The Ripper? He was the Ripper? And someone killed him?"

"Yeah. I'm surprised you didn't hear anything. It's been all over the TV." He leaned toward Oliver and lowered his voice, one expert to another. "This hasn't made the papers yet, so don't go spreading it around, but you should have seen the guy. Somebody dressed him up like a deer, then hacked him to death. He looked like a pack of dogs had been at him."

"How horrible!"

"Yeah, not what you'd call your typical death by knifing. Somebody put a lot of planning and a lot of rage into that."

Somebody who had taken great pains to remove any sign of his presence. Oliver had no fears in that regard. His pulse was steady, his voice perfectly normal. "I should imagine. A deer!"

"And the worst thing is," McCaffrey went on, "I thought I recognized the setup. That's why I'm here." Oliver's heart stuttered. "You got a copy of Bullfinch's Mythology?"

Oh. Oliver smiled broadly. "Of course. This way, please."

He guided McCaffrey to the classical section, and handed him a paperback edition. McCaffrey riffled through to the index. "Funny, the things that'll stick in a kid's head," he said. "I know I've heard the story. The guy who got turned into a deer and killed by his dogs. What was his name? Acheron, Atticus—"

"Actaeon."

Oliver knew it was a mistake the second it left his lips — by his own sudden chill, and by the sad but steely look that came into McCaffrey's tight eyes. The detective slid the book back onto the shelf. "Yeah, that was it. Actaeon. Y'know, I don't think there's two people in this whole city who'd know that so offhand."

"It's the educational system." Oliver retreated to the counter, his island of security. McCaffrey was right behind him. Through the window Oliver saw the two officers, no longer lounging, watching the store. "They don't promote the classics anymore. So few people have any sense of the richness of our literary heritage. It's an absolute crime."

"Ain't it, though? Doubt if I would've got into mythology myself, if I hadn't been so hot on those old sword-and-sandal epics. But the minute I saw the body, I remembered the story. Actaeon. The guy who insulted Diana." He gazed over Oliver's head to the "gallery," to the drawing of the goddess with a dead girl's face. "What happened, Mike?" he said, almost gently. "He beat you to the punch?"

"He was a barbarian," Oliver spat. "No talent. No sense of aesthetics. Those people are a blight on humanity's soul."

"That's not up to us to judge. You're going to have to come down to the station, Mr. Hewitt. I'd like to ask you about a few things."

Oliver slumped. It wasn't so bad, getting caught by a critic. At least the man had some appreciation for the classics. "Will I need a lawyer?"

"Yeah, I'd say so. We've got a couple partial prints the boys are anxious to identify. There's also a witness who can place you at the scene around the time of the murder." He took Oliver by the arm, in a firm but understanding grip. "You can call from the station. I'll read you your rights in the car."

"Thank you."

The two policemen stood at alert while Oliver locked the bookstore door behind him, McCaffrey at his back. "One thing, Detective," Oliver said. "Please don't judge me by that last night. It wasn't my best work."

\<Birth of an Idea\>
Keith Gouveia

Peter sat at his kitchen table, his paints and brushes neatly placed in front of him as he delicately scraped off the tarter and calcium buildup around his newest trophy. A photo of the young woman he and Mike butchered last night off to his left. Both had taken their respective trophies from her.

Mike broke the silence blanketing the room as he entered with the morning newspaper unfolded in his hands. "Another killer was caught," he said, laying the paper out across the circular table, almost knocking over Peter's small bottles of paint.

With a sigh, Peter placed his tools down. With his hands balled into fists, he asked, "What am I doing right now?"

Mike's gaze shifted to the side. "Working."

"And what have I told you about disturbing me while I'm working?"

"Not to," he said, still refusing to look him in the eye.

Peter slammed his fist down on the table. "This isn't a finger I just toss into a zip-lock bag and throw on ice, you know. This is art! I need to concentrate, not coddle a two year old."

"I'm sorry, really sorry." Mike finally locked his gaze on Peter. "This news is disheartening as it seems to be happening more and more. The police and feds are catching on too quickly…and it's got me thinking. They all worked alone—"

"I'm beginning to think that's the way to go," said Peter with a half-smile.

"Be serious. How many men and women are out there right now, desperate and alone?"

"If they're desperate, then that means they screwed up."

"Exactly. This guy made a simple mistake and it cost him. How do we know we're not making the same mistakes?"

"Experience," he answered, voice cold and flat.

"And maybe that's all our brethren need…experience."

Peter leaned forward in his chair. "Little late for him."

"In all walks of life there's a community. A place to hang your head with like-minded people. We need a place like that for us."

"We're not like-minded people," he said, relaxing in his chair. "We're murderers with different—"

"Look," Mike said, pointing at a black and white photo of a crime scene. "He's an artist, just like you. We all have more in common than you'll admit."

Peter leaned forward again and eyed the photo. "Not like me," he said, leaning back. "He's a sculptor."

"Semantics, Peter. He made a stupid mistake and hung sketches of his kills in his store, a mistake you'd never let me make."

"Damn right!"

"If he had a safe place to hang them, he'd still be out there. And hey, you could finally show off your talent to a more…sophisticated audience than I."

The wide toothy grin sickened him. Helping others was beyond his understanding. He was a predator. But Mike had just said the one thing that could persuade him, and he knew it. With a deep breath, he said, "And how do you propose we do that? This isn't alcoholics anonymous, this is murder!"

"It can be done. What about online? We can make a website where killers from all around the world can come together for moral support, share tips and tricks of the trade, and just provide an overall sense of camaraderie. Killing doesn't have to be a solitary sport."

"Like a forum?" Peter asked. "You know how much work it'll be to keep such a thing secret?"

Mike crossed his arms, a sign he was getting frustrated. "We don't want to keep it a secret. We just want to keep it untraceable...like those sites that post snuff films."

"Untraceable..." Peter mumbled, more to himself than to Mike.

Peter realized how good an idea it actually was, though he would not—could not—let Mike know that. Over the years they had killed forty-three people of various race and creed. Most of their victims had been from chance encounters like the coffee shop bitch who had lost her cool with a barista, or the police officer who tasered a teenage girl because she spit at him. However, when the monotony of the nine to five grew unbearable, they went out looking for trouble. Forty-three was a far cry above the average serial killer, and it was a testament of their partnership, one that could benefit countless others.

"Think you can do it?"

Peter's tongue glided over his upper teeth as he refrained from taking insult. "And what do you call such a thing?"

"I don't know," Mike said as his arms dropped to his sides, "Murder club?"

"No, man, that's so...generic."

"Lynch Mob? The Killer Society?"

Just like everything else, Mike just tossed out his random ideas with little thought or imagination and that irked him.

"How about," Peter paused, contemplating the idea, "The Snuff Syndicate?"

Mike's eyes went wide with enthusiasm. "Oh, I like it." He nodded. "When I'm done here, we'll go shopping."

"Oh, I can't wait," Mike said, rubbing his hands together.

Peter returned his attention to the tooth. He needed a polished surface to paint Julie's portrait on. It was delicate and painstaking work, but he loved it. Only a select few in the world had a hand steady enough to paint such minute drawings. His parents had wanted him to be a doctor, had sent him to the University of Central Florida to study, but he had other desires. Other ambitions. He dropped out, but in some regard, he utilized those skills taught in those three semesters of pre-med.

A whoosh of air escaping Mike's nostrils broke Peter's concentration. Peter looked up to see that childish, 'I got what I wanted' look upon Mike's face.

"Why are you still here?"

"How long do you think you'll be?"

Peter felt his jaw go slack. "Are you serious?"

"You can paint that anytime. Our brothers and sisters in blood need us now."

"Fine," Peter replied, placing the tooth and his tools down on the table. "We'll do it now, but if you don't stop being so melodramatic it'll be your tooth I'm polishing next."

Mike smiled. "Like I've never heard that one before."

<Tipping the Odds>
Carey Burns

He didn't remember how he even got on the subject, but Ronald Benson stood in front of his students and relayed the story about his ransacked Vegas hotel room. His nervous laughter sounded like a hyena trying to keep quiet in church and the group of students looked confused and perhaps a bit scared.

"It turned out I left my spare room key in the casino and some meth addict found it and tried all the doors until he found my room…all the way on the sixth floor." Ronald stood behind the podium, wishing he hadn't strayed from the lesson plan. Bad things happened when he did.

His students stood as the minute hand finally stopped on the ten, releasing them from Mathematics Convention Story Hell. They all made a mad dash for the door, eager to put as much distance between them and the pointless musings of a math geek as they could, except for one.

She was a pretty redhead that sat in the front row. She waited until the initial press of students had passed and gathered her books and clutched them to her chest, shyly creeping toward the lectern. "Professor Benson, I know you're busy, but I was wondering if you might be able to just look at my assignment and let me know if I did it right."

Ronald studied her shoulders, the thin straps of her tank top barely covering the fuchsia straps of her brassiere. He forced his gaze from her creamy skin and stared into her blue eyes. "Yes, uh, what is it you're having trouble with?"

The girl set her books on his desk and pointed at a sheet of notebook paper. "Everything. See, math really isn't my thing. I barely passed College Algebra before transferring here and no matter how many times I read the book, I just don't think I'm getting Stats." She frowned.

It was torture for him not to look at her firm, round breasts held captive by the scrap of fabric, but he resisted, focusing on the numbers on the paper instead. It was all wrong. "You're not quite there, but you're on the right track."

He closed his eyes and took a breath then looked up into her eyes again. "I have office hours tomorrow, you can stop in and we can go over the assignment."

Her eyelashes fluttered and she smiled. "Oh. Okay. What time should I come by?"

She's flirting with me, he thought and matched her smile with his own, nervously tucking his hair behind his ear. "Anytime between ten and noon is fine. I'm on the third floor."

"I'm sure I'll find it." She scooped up her books and hurried to the door.

Ronald watched her leave, a glimmer of hope making him smile even wider. A pretty thing like her batting her eyelashes at me.

As the next group of students crowded at the door, he shoved his books into his briefcase and strode through them out into the hallway. He had a good feeling about her as he headed to his office.

"Think, Ronnie, think! What is her name?" he asked the ceiling, his brow creased in thought. Finally, he pulled the roster from his briefcase and scanned the names, pleased that the redhead was one of only four girls in the class. He closed his eyes, thinking back to the start of class when he took attendance and imagined her raising her hand and calling out "Here."

"Higgins! Emily Higgins!" He laughed, clearing a stack of papers from the chair opposite his own.

Ronald tidied up the rest of his office for when she stopped by to visit.

The next morning he showered and shaved and combed his sandy brown hair, parting it on the right and wishing his long bangs weren't so wavy. He opened his closet and marveled at how orderly it looked: twelve pairs of similar tan pants all hung side by side on identical white plastic hangers and twelve identical butter yellow polo shirts filled out the rest of his wardrobe. He chose a shirt and a pair of pants and completed his outfit with his only pair of brown leather loafers.

Once dressed, he took the bus to campus, arriving just before ten o'clock. His office was just across the busy main street and he waited at the crosswalk desperately pressing the button until it finally gave him the right of way and he dashed across the street to the math building.

Ronald sprinted up the stairwell to the third floor, eager to see Emily. As he rounded the corner to his office, he stopped in mid-step: the hallway was empty.

With a sigh, he unlocked his office door and settled in behind his desk. Where could she be? He imagined her wandering the hallways on the third floor, searching for his door. He booted up his computer and checked his email to see if maybe she sent him a message explaining her lateness, his heart sinking in his empty inbox.

Finally at 11:30 he heard a soft knock on his door and his heart beat so hard he felt almost queasy. "Come in." He tried to look calm and relaxed, like he hadn't been worrying for over 45 minutes.

The door opened and Emily stepped inside, a vision in her hot pink tank top and short black skirt. "Hi, Professor Benson."

He smiled. "Hello, it's Emily, isn't it? Please, have a seat." He gestured at the chair in front of him.

She perched on the edge of the seat and kept her books on her lap, a polite smile on her lips. "I stayed up all night working on the assignment and I think I finally figured out what I've been doing wrong." Emily pulled a sheet of yellow legal paper out of a folder and handed it to Ronald, his fingertips grazing hers as he reached for it and she trembled.

While he studied her neat handwriting, he breathed in her sweet, fruity perfume. At first glance he could tell everything added up, but he took his time examining her work, not wanting to rush her away so soon.

Finally, he smiled and folded his hands over the paper. "I'm impressed. Tell me, how did it come to you?"

Her pale cheeks blushed a light pink. "Honestly, my boyfriend helped me. He had Stats with Zimmermann last semester so he knew the material."

Boyfriend. That one word pierced his heart and he plucked the paper from the desktop and slid it toward Emily, his lips pinched into a frown. "So, he helped you figure it all out then or he did the work for you?"

"He just helped me." Her cheeks paled at his accusation and her eyes misted over. "He explained it so I could actually understand it. It is my work, Professor Benson."

Ronald glared at her. "Then why did you bother coming to my office and wasting my time if you have it all figured out?"

"I…I didn't want to be rude by not showing up. I was just being nice."

Nice. Ronald stared at Emily with his cold brown eyes and folded his hands on his desk. "I'll see you in class tomorrow then."

Emily blinked back tears and tucked the paper into her folder and rose to leave, mumbling, "Thank you, Professor." She stepped into the hallway and shut the door behind her.

Her sickeningly sweet perfume hung in the air choking him and Ronald trembled, his calm façade crumbling with each whiff of her scent. She was one of those girls.

His mind flashed back to high school, to his first love Becky O'Dell. She was smart and pretty and he thought she liked him, but then she said the fateful words: I don't like you that way; I was just being nice to you. He was crushed, so he smashed her head in with a rock.

Ronald licked his lips and clenched his fists as he thought about all the others. Each time he thought he might have a chance, they would rebuff him, say they were just being nice to him. The nice girls were worse than the ones that would tell him 'No' straightaway. They shouldn't have led him on like that. He didn't deserve it. He worked himself into a frenzy, thinking about the first date; the first kiss; the first night of passion. All the possibilities, and now, none of it would see fruition.

The words of his second victim, Tina, a girl from his English Comp class freshman year at college filled his ears. *I felt sorry for you.* Ronald pressed the heels of his palms against his closed eyes, his anger swelling in his veins until all he could hear was the swoosh-swoosh of his pulse.

Emily would have to learn a hard lesson.

The rest of the day Ronald's brain shifted into automatic statistics mode. He gave in-class assignments and sat at his desk, plotting. He dismissed them all early so he could continue to think and theorize and plan. Just like with his other victims, he set out to make the probability of him, Ronald Benson, being a suspect in Emily's murder nil. After seven kills and zero encounters with the police, he was confident he could kill just about anybody and get away with it.

He settled into his office and came up with a timetable first. Except for his first two kills, he always created one so that he could not only prepare for the kill, but also distance himself from the victim so that he wouldn't be part of an initial inquiry. He'd sometimes wait a full year before finally carrying out his deadly task just so he couldn't be connected with her. With Amber, his third, he waited a year and a half after he quit working with her at Denny's before killing her. Veronica, his former neighbor, hadn't lived in his apartment complex in over thirteen months when he killed her.

He would come up with a murder weapon next, knowing that the odds of him getting caught increased if he repeated the same weapon or left similar injuries on his victims. After that first rock to the skull, he stabbed, strangled, drowned, poisoned, pushed and buried alive.

Exhausted, he called it a day and locked up his office. He mulled over every mode of death he could think of, trying to find that perfect fit and as Ronald crossed the street to the bus stop he settled on something more personal, squeezing the life from Emily Higgins' exposed neck.

Back at home in his studio apartment, Ronald set three sheets of plain white computer paper side by side on his coffee table. He sat on the floor, legs crossed Indian style and picked up a pencil. The yellow Dixon Ticonderoga had planned the deaths of all seven girls and Ronald smiled. The pencil would never talk.

Ronald wrote in his perfect block script at the top of the first page 'X<10; X>5'. This meant anytime between May and October he could strike and the odds are he would not be a suspect. He wouldn't have Emily in either Spring or Summer semester so he wouldn't automatically be a suspect. If he could avoid contact with her all that time, he'd be in the clear.

Next, he wrote 'Y=EC'. He would steal an extension cord and that would be what he would use to strangle her. He thought back to Amber and how he had used her own pink silk scarf to choke her, but that was across the country and over fifteen years ago. No one would make the connection between the two girls.

Ronald filled the three sheets with detailed, coded notes that to anyone else would look like a math teacher's inane scribbling. 'G' stood for gloves and 'C' stood for cap and 'Z'; well 'Z' was Ronald.

As the semester came to a close, Ronald breathed a sigh of relief that Emily Higgins earned a C. He was fully prepared to pass her just so that he wouldn't have to revise his timeline. Something about her vacant smile from the front row during class made him want to get it over with as soon as possible and if that meant giving her fictitious extra credit to squeak by, so be it. She'd be dead before graduation anyway so what did it matter?

Ronald spent all of winter break visualizing his plan. He would find out where she lived from his old class roster and he'd check out the building frequently to make sure she still lived there and to learn her day-by-day patterns.

Emily didn't have a car so Ronald found himself following her on foot from a safe distance to see where she worked. He tracked her to the Olive Garden and quickly learned she was working nights and weekends and she'd either walk or ride her bicycle home. After following her for a few days, he switched up to parking his car across the street from her apartment building and watching her come and go. It was easy to track her schedule and learn the usual routes she took.

Ronald learned Emily's school schedule by logging into the school's student record system as the department secretary. She had one password for everything and she kept it written down on her desk blotter for the world to see. He made sure to check the schedule from a colleague's office, just in case.

When classes resumed, Ronald settled into an easy pattern of school, following Emily, and waiting. At night he parked across the street from her apartment building and waited for her to turn the light off before heading home. She lived with another girl and he'd sometimes see them head out for a run together and he'd have to duck down in the driver's seat of his car so they wouldn't see him.

By early February Ronald's obsession pained him. He fought the urges to call her or run into her, a problem he'd never had before. It worried him that he might let affection or desire get in the way of what he needed to do and when Valentine's Day came he felt depressed and alone. He decided to get out of his apartment and treat himself to a nice dinner out.

He drove to a little Thai place down the street and stood in line behind several couples until the hostess ushered him to a small table for one in the center of the restaurant. He felt pitying eyes from every table, but sat down to enjoy a meal. As he studied the menu he happened to glance to his right and nearly fell off his chair as he locked eyes with Emily who was with her boyfriend.

He felt sick and scared, angry with her for being with someone else and with himself for not being thorough enough to avoid the accidental encounter. Panicked, he weighed his options and sprang to his feet, dropping his napkin on the table as he bolted for the door.

The hostess stared at him in disbelief as he squeezed past her and another couple at the entrance.

"Thank you," he called over his shoulder and disappeared through the door.

Outside, Ronald took several gulps of air to slow his frantic heartbeat and walked calmly to his car. He opened the door and sat down, the heavy door swinging shut with a 'clunk.' As he started it up and pulled away from the restaurant, he thought about how beautiful she looked.

Ronald went into damage control mode for the next month, only driving past her apartment three times a week and parking outside the Olive Garden a handful of times. He was careful so he wouldn't get caught or accidentally see her again, but he couldn't stop thinking about the teal v-neck sweater she wore that night and the way her blue eyes sparkled in the candlelight. Definitely strangling her.

As he grew more relaxed, he stepped up his visits. One night in April, after a restless night's sleep, he dozed off in his car in the Olive Garden's parking lot. He woke with a jolt, unsure of where he was until he saw the building straight ahead. The lot was vacant and the lights were off and Ronald's heartbeat turned into a sprint when he saw it was well after midnight. Not only had he missed seeing her, he drew attention to himself and his car. This could increase the odds of him being a suspect.

Worried, he called in sick for the next three days, confining himself to his apartment while he struggled to clean up the damage he had done. It was clear that now he would have to wait until November so enough time would pass. Nobody would remember seeing him after seven months, let alone connect it to Emily's death. If the police ever questioned him, he would just say he had too much to drink at the bar down the street and he decided to pull into the parking lot to sleep it off. Everything would be okay. Still, he didn't drive by her apartment or even go near the restaurant for a few weeks.

As finals came to an end, Ronald's colleagues invited him to a retirement dinner for Max, one of the algebra professors. He tried to beg out of it, but they insisted, so he piled into the minivan along with the group.

Ronald shifted on the seat, uneasy with the feeling of being at the mercy of another person's whims. When the van finally pulled into the parking lot of the Olive Garden, he wanted to run.

"Are you sure you want to eat here?" he asked, reluctantly climbing out of the van.

"Yeah, we come here all the time. The food is good and it's fairly priced." Max, the retiree smiled, clapping Ronald on the shoulder.

He followed his peers into the restaurant and glanced around, searching for any sign of Emily. He knew she would be there and as the hostess seated them at a large, round table he saw her laughing with another waitress across the room. He hid behind his menu, praying that she would not see him.

After a few moments he heard her voice. "Good evening, gentlemen, my name's Emily, and I'll be serving you tonight. May I start you out with any drinks or appetizers?"

Ronald tried to steady his hold on the menu while the others ordered and when it was his turn he croaked. "Just water, thank you."

"Professor Benson?" she asked.

He forced a smile and lowered the menu and gave her his most genuine quizzical look. "Yes, do I know you?"

Her red lips parted slightly and fell into a frown. "I was in your stats class last semester."

Ronald studied her face, trying to look like he couldn't quite place her. "Were you in my two o'clock session?"

"No, one o'clock."

He smiled. "I'm sorry. It is nice to see you though."

"That's okay," she shrugged, "I'll be right back with your drinks."

Ronald kept his cool for the rest of the night, catching the scent of her perfume when she hovered close to his shoulder to serve him. Although he enjoyed his colleagues' company, he knew he couldn't join them again, but he was happy to see and speak with Emily.

Later that week Emily moved out of her apartment and her parents arrived to take her home for the summer, sending Ronald into panic mode.

He checked her fall schedule at least once a week, hoping she would return to school and list a new address, but June passed and turned into July without any activity on her account. Finally, the last week of July Emily listed a new address and registered for a full load of classes.

It was easy to find the small house and Ronald couldn't believe his luck. A seven foot privacy fence surrounded it on three sides and a huge, overgrown hedge hid the front of the house. He watched the house from the park across the street, awaiting her return.

On the first day of August Emily moved in. Ronald sat on a bench in the park, pretending to read a newspaper as he watched her parents pull out of the driveway while she waved farewell from the front door. At long last, Emily was alone.

Ronald felt bolder and spent more time in the park. He'd sit for hours on the bench, his eyes hidden behind dark sunglasses as he pretended to read a book. He knew she was working again, but not at the Olive Garden. He tracked her one night to a Ruby Tuesday's and watched her for a few weeks, memorizing her schedule. He often wondered how she managed to work five or six days a week and still manage a full course load.

Just before the semester began Ronald followed Emily to a Middle Eastern restaurant and decided to go in and place an order to go, just to see her up close. He lined up behind a college student that smelled of patchouli oil and studied the back of her head. As he fantasized about touching her soft earlobe with his fingers, she turned around.

Her eyes flashed open wide as she recognized him. "Oh, hi, Professor. How are you?"

Ronald's cheeks flushed a light pink. "Hi there, uh, oh give me a minute…"

She scowled. "It's Emily. I'm sure you remember me."

"Oh, yes, Emily. I'm well, how are you?"

"Fine thanks." She shifted her weight from foot to foot and she glanced up to the right, searching the air for something to say. "So, are you ready for classes to start?"

He smiled, focusing on her blue eyes. "Oh, I suspect it will be the same as the last semester. How about you, do you have a full load of classes?"

Her eyelashes fluttered. "Yes." She turned her head as the woman behind the register asked for her order and said, "I guess I'm next."

Ronald listened as she ordered and closed his eyes, whispering, "Yes, you are."

With less than three months to go Ronald avoided all contact with Emily. He may run the risk of missing a change in her schedule and as much as he wanted to drive down her street or sit in the park, he knew he had to keep out of her life so he wouldn't bring unwanted attention to himself.

In September he had to go out of state for a conference and as he walked down the hallway of the hotel he noticed a maintenance cart in the hallway. The sight of a bright orange extension cord bundled up on the floor brought a smile to his lips. Ronald looked around for any sign of video cameras, maintenance workers or guests and when he was sure he was alone, he snatched it up and stuffed it into his jacket. He would cut the ends off the cord when he returned home so that he'd have a nice four foot piece and dispose of the leftovers.

There was a Good Will store a few blocks from his hotel and Ronald stopped in one evening, searching for a dark sweat suit he could wear and dispose of easily. He cruised the color-separated racks until he found a dark evergreen set in a XXL size, much larger than his thin frame needed, but it would throw off the police if they ever found the clothes. He slipped the cashier a five dollar bill and left without a bag or receipt, tucking the clothes under his arm.

On the last day of the convention he stuffed the cord into his baggage and headed for the airport. If they searched his bag and asked him about the cord, he would tell them that a colleague had forgotten it after a presentation and he was bringing it back for him.

As he approached the counter he practiced his response, but he didn't have to worry. The clerk slipped a tracking sticker over the bag's handle and hefted it onto the conveyor belt, sending it off to be loaded into the belly of the plane.

Ronald napped during the three hour flight, dreaming of what he would say to Emily in her final moments. He awoke refreshed and ready to conquer the world.

Mid-October Ronald felt his conviction waver when he happened to see Emily through the window at Borders, sitting at a table reading a magazine. He ducked his head and sneaked a glance at her and when he spied the cover he scurried away. It was "Modern Bride."

He hurried down the street, his guts aflame with anger and jealousy. He wanted to kill her right then, but he'd spoil everything if he did that.

Instead, he stopped at the grocery store and strode over to the magazine display, searching for his own copy of Emily's magazine. He snatched it up, checked out at the self-service register and hurried home.

Once in the safety of his apartment, he flipped through

the pages, wondering what dress she dreamed of while sitting at the bookstore. He stopped a few pages in, stunned to see a thin, pale redhead in a body-hugging, full-length sequined gown. He searched a drawer for a pair of scissors, carefully cut the bride free from the page and made her dance like a puppet on the coffee table.

He soon grew tired of her, pulled a black pen from his briefcase and made little X's over her eyes. With a smile and lighter heart, he left the doll on the table and walked over to the kitchen to start dinner.

On the first of November, Ronald felt in his gut that the day was near. He stole a pair of heavy duty rubberized gloves from a hardware store and washed them to clear away any powders, residues, or fingerprints and set them aside in a plastic shopping bag. Ronald washed the extension cord too and put it in a drawer, worried that it would seem suspicious for all the items to be in the same bag.

He hid the small bride picture on the top of the refrigerator, but he needed to dispose of the rest of the magazine because police would find it odd if they ever came to his apartment and found a bridal magazine. After much thought, he wiped each page with a cloth to clear away any prints and removed each page from the glued spine. He took the loose pages to the school and fed them into the shredder outside his office door. Later, he took the bag of shreds to a secluded spot by the river and burned every last wisp of paper. Ronald threw the severed spine of the magazine away in a garbage can outside a movie theater two towns over.

While there he saw a wig shop and stopped outside the window, smiling when he saw a toupee that looked just like his own hair. *I have to shave my head so no hairs end up as evidence anyway, I should buy it,* he thought, screwing up the courage to go inside. With a deep breath he went inside.

"Yes, sir, may I help you?" a young woman with short blond hair asked.

Ronald pointed at the toupee. "I want to buy that." He saw her brow arch in curiosity. "I was diagnosed with cancer and have to have treatments, so I'll need a wig. I saw that one and it is perfect, don't you think?"

The girl frowned. "I'm so sorry to hear that." She went to the window and snatched up the white Styrofoam head that displayed the wig. "Would you like to try it on? You should make sure it'll fit before you buy it." She slipped the wig from the head and fluffed the hair.

"Um...no, I'd rather not. See, I just got the news and that might make it too real." He lied, just wanting to get out of the store.

She nodded. "I understand. Well, you keep your receipt and if it turns out you need a different piece, you just come on in." She carefully put the wig into a paper box and started to put it in a bag.

"No, that's okay. I don't like plastic bags. Wasteful. And I'm sure it'll be fine. I don't need a receipt." He handed her cash and held out his palm for his change. "Have a good day."

"Bye." She watched him leave, shaking her head in pity.

On a clear, brisk day just before Thanksgiving, Ronald woke and decided to put his plan into action. He showered and shaved his arms, armpits, chest, legs and back careful not to miss any hair or knick his skin. He stood, naked and hairless and stared at his damp hair in the mirror. With a sigh, he lifted a pair of clippers, pressed the on switch and guided the metal blade to his scalp, its low hum growing deeper with every swath, he cut through his hair. In minutes, bald Ronald was sweeping up the clippings and stuffing them into a paper bag. He pulled his toupee onto his pale scalp and adjusted it so that it looked natural.

Ronald returned to his bedroom and pulled on a pair of white briefs and a white t-shirt then opened his closet and took out a pair of Dockers and a yellow polo. Once dressed, he took an old backpack he had stolen from a bus stop and stuffed the dark green sweat suit into it along with the rubber gloves, a pair of white cotton gloves, and the extension cord.

With everything in place, he fetched the bag of hair and slid one strap of the backpack over his shoulder and opened the apartment door. He stepped out and glanced down the hall and when he saw he was alone; he locked the door and hurried down to the stairwell and out into the sunshine.

He had to be careful. He had to strike the right balance of being noticed to form his alibi and being invisible so he wouldn't get caught. Ronald drove to a coffee shop and disposed of the bag of hair in a garbage can outside then spent an hour reading a newspaper and drinking a cup of black coffee. Next, he drove to the grocery store, taking his time in each aisle, finally leaving with several cans of soup, boxes of macaroni and cheese, and four rolls of toilet paper as well as a receipt with the date and time on it.

Ronald checked his watch and smiled. It wouldn't be long now.

He parked his car three streets away from Emily's house and pulled the sweatpants on over his Dockers, the elastic ankles catching on his shoes. Ronald squirmed in the driver's seat until the sweatpants were on and he pulled the drawstring tight, making sure to knot it. With a sigh, he plucked the toupee from his head and stuffed it under the seat then pulled the hooded sweatshirt over his head. He stole a look at himself in the rearview mirror and smiled. With his hood up, he didn't even look like himself.

Ronald closed his eyes and remembered the day in his office that led to what he was about to do and his calm outer shell crumbled as his hatred of her flushed his cheeks and burned his eyes. She'd suffer just like the others.

He opened the car door and strolled down the sidewalk,

the street empty and nobody around to notice him. He turned down her street, ducking into the large hedge at the end of her yard. He crossed the yard to the back of the house, knowing every step he took was hidden by the privacy fence and the hedge.

The sound of Fleetwood Mac came from inside the house and he knew she would be getting ready for work. He crept toward the backdoor and chuckled, thinking how that privacy fence was a godsend.

Ronald opened his backpack and the zipper made a soft ripping noise. He pulled out the cotton gloves and eased his hands inside them then pulled on the heavier rubber gloves and returned the backpack to his shoulder. He turned the doorknob, breath held captive in his chest until the door opened.

Inside, he crept through the small kitchen and stopped. The hum of her hairdryer masked any noise he made. He strolled into the living room and as he passed the stereo, he turned up the music so any sound of her struggle would be drowned out. Ronald stepped closer to the bathroom door where Emily was drying her red hair.

With a contented smile he reached into his bag and pulled out the orange cord and set the bag on the floor. He held the cord in his hands, holding it taught as he ducked into her bedroom and hid behind the door.

The smell of her perfume filled his nose, sweet and delicious while he waited for her to come into her bedroom. A chill of adrenaline shivered down his back as he marveled at the perfection of his day. She would be utterly surprised and have no idea who her attacker was unless he spoke, which he decided he wouldn't do. She deserved no explanation from him.

Ronald breathed soft, quick breaths as Emily turned off the hairdryer. He listened as she flushed the toilet and hummed along with the music, anticipating the moment.

His pink tongue flicked out to moisten his lips and he heard the bathroom door open and the tread of her feet on the carpet just on the other side of the door.

With one fluid motion he stepped forward as she entered the bedroom and lifted the cord up over her head then pulled it to her neck, forcing her against his chest as she tried to lurch forward to escape.

Ronald pulled the cord tighter, her frantic fingers unable to pull it free as she sputtered and flailed. He arched his back and pulled up on the cord, lifting her off her feet and the crunch of broken vertebrae brought a smile to his lips. When Emily's body went limp, he held her, suspended for a full five minutes, just to make sure she was dead. He inhaled the smell of her clean, dry hair then released his grip and let her fall in a heap at his feet, her dead eyes staring under her dresser.

He stood tall, the weight that held him down for nearly a year lifted and he felt alive again. He stepped over her body and stuffed his cord and rubber gloves into the backpack and walked through the living room into the kitchen and out the back door.

As he peered out from the hedge, he tucked the cotton gloves in the pack and zipped it up, slipping the straps over his shoulders. With the coast clear, he stepped out onto the sidewalk and sauntered down the street back to his car. He reveled in how easy Emily's murder was, much smoother and less messy than the others. He'd done all he could to keep the odds in his favor of not being caught and now, he'd take off his sweats and go celebrate.

Classes resumed after Thanksgiving break and Ronald's world returned to normal. When news broke about Emily's brutal murder, he remained calm and didn't do anything to rouse suspicion, not even when the police called him at home and invited him to the station to answer a few questions.

He sat in the interrogation room, hands folded neatly on the desk and waited for the detective to begin.

"Mr. Benson, did you know Emily Higgins?"

He frowned and nodded, false sympathy in his eyes. "Yes, she was a student of mine. Nice girl, she didn't quite grasp the material at first, but she pulled through in the end."

He shifted his striped tie and leaned his forearms on the desk. "Did you ever have any encounters with Miss Higgins outside of the classroom?"

"Encounters?" He feigned shock. "No. I did bump into her a few times at restaurants, but that's it."

"Hmm. See, the reason I ask is when we searched Miss Higgins' house we found this journal." He moved a file folder and revealed a brown leather-bound book and opened it, flipping the pages toward the back. "There's a piece of paper here with your name on it."

Ronald tilted his head to the left and peered at the yellow sheet of paper, curious about its contents. "Really?"

"Yep. Here, take a look." He slid the paper toward Ronald and studied his face.

Ronald read Emily's neat handwriting, trying not to show surprise. It was a simple note with 'Professor Benson' centered at the top with four dated entries below, a chronicle of the times Ronald had screwed up and allowed himself to be seen. He studied it for a moment and met the detective's accusing gaze. "I don't understand. Why would she write this?"

"There's more..." He flipped to another page in the book and studied Ronald's expression.

Surprise isn't quite the word for what creased Ronald's brow as he read his name over and over on the page. He reached forward and touched the page, confused, then lifted it to see his class times and office hours written in pink ink on the next page.

"Professor, it appears Miss Higgins may have been focused on you." The detective opened the file folder and slid out three pencil sketches of Ronald's face.

"Focused? I..." What did this mean? Did Emily actually like him? *What have I done?*

The detective cleared his throat. "I'm so sorry that we had to bring you down here like this, sir. We just needed to see if you may have known anything."

"I understand...this is all so bizarre. Do you have a suspect?" He blinked a few times, still trying to process Emily's scribblings.

"Yeah. We're thinking it might be the boyfriend. Off the record, of course." He stacked the sketches on top of the folder and stood to leave.

"Of course." Ronald stood and ran his hand through his hair.

The detective smiled and crossed the room to open the door. "Like I said, sorry to drop all of this on you. It must be pretty unsettling to find out someone has been watching you and following you without you even knowing."

Ronald faked a smile. "You have no idea."

<Bound By Blood>
Keith Gouveia

"Ugh!" Mike jolted forward, startled by the vision of Max Frinkle and his goons standing over him, pointing and laughing, calling him names like sicko and freak.

His breath caught in his throat as his heart pounded like thunder in his chest. Sweat covered every inch of him. Slowly, as his eyes adjusted to the darkness, his breaths became shorter. Controlled.

Mouth dry, he pulled his tongue free from the roof of his mouth, the stinging sensation lasting the briefest of seconds. He reached over to the nightstand for a drink, but then remembered he hadn't brought a glass of water to bed with him. *The one time I need it.*

With a deep sigh, Mike threw the light blanket off his naked form and swung his legs over the edge. His feet probed the hardwood floor for his slippers and when they found them, he stood and walked over to the door for his robe.

He walked to the kitchen in need of a drink. *That day represents a turning point in my life, why does it haunt me so?*

It was freshman year at Timber Creek High School when he met Peter for the first time. Mike had been walking to school when he happened upon the carcass of a dog at the side of the road. Curious, he stepped up to it and knelt down beside it. The beast's abdomen was split open with its intestines spilled; the side of its face devoid of fur, a crimson smear of flesh and scattered pebbles. It was beautiful.

As he reached a shaky finger toward a coiled section of tubular tissue, Max Frinkle made his presence known.

"You sick, perverted, fuck!"

Mike felt the boy's powerful hands at his back and he fell forward, his face falling into the gore that lay spread out across the street.

"Ewe," said one of Max's thugs. "That's so gross!"

"Are you happy now, freak?" Max asked.

Mike rolled over to face his tormentors, the metallic taste of blood on his lips.

Max's buddies erupted into laughter at the sight of his blood-smeared face, then their laughter turned into a chant. "Freak! Freak! Freak!"

"Is the little freak going to cry?" Max asked, then was suddenly spun around and leveled by a right hook to the side of his jaw.

Max fell to the ground beside Mike, his head bouncing back on impact with the pavement. Mouths hung open in disbelief, eyes wide and fixated on the stranger dressed in blue jeans and a black *KISS* T-shirt.

"Anyone else need their clock cleaned?" he asked, his voice filled with confidence and strength Mike could only admire.

Max's so-called friends bolted, leaving him there half in the road and unconscious.

Mike remained silent. Countless scenarios playing out in his fractured mind. Images of Peter spinning around and pummeling him, of the boy pointing and laughing, and worst of all, of him simply walking away never to speak to him again.

"Are you all right?" the boy asked, extending his hand toward him.

Mike accepted the gesture and got to his feet before replying, "Yeah."

"You gotta name?"

"M-Mike."

"Nice to meet you, I'm Peter," said the boy as he turned and stared down at the dead dog.

"You go to Timber High?"

Mike could only nod in response.

"We should probably get you cleaned up," Peter finally said.

"I'll wash up at school. We should go. We don't want to be here when he wakes up."

Peter took one last look at his handiwork, then nodded. "The dog's pretty cool though, huh?"

Mike felt his eyes go wide. "Yeah, it was!"

As they walked to school, Peter talked to Mike in a manner he was not accustomed to, one of respect and understanding. He wasn't disturbed by the mask of blood Mike wore, nor did he tease him about it.

By the time the two had to go their separate ways for class, Mike had learned Peter moved to Florida from Massachusetts over the summer; loved Rock and Heavy Metal Bands; and was a horror movie buff who also found time to enjoy Spider-Man comics. All in all, best friend material.

There was only 40 minutes left in the school day when Mike asked to be excused from Math to go to the bathroom. On his way there, he heard Max's unmistakable voice. He sounded as if he were trying to keep his voice down so as not to be overheard, but threatening as well. Mike investigated and found Peter pinned to the wall, a trail of blood trickling down his lip from his nose and a small lump upon his forehead.

Mike tip-toed closer, and it looked as though Peter had spotted him, but remained quiet about his presence and seemed to goad his attacker with an accusatory finger and mockery. Max had Peter at the top of the staircase and Mike feared one wrong move on Max's part and his newfound friend would accidentally slip and tumble down the concrete steps.

He was able to get right up behind Max and when the bully removed his hands from Peter's T-shirt in an effort to deliver one last blow, Mike shoved his hands into Max with all his might. The boy fell over down the steps and slammed his head. His neck buckled up at the base with a crack, and his body slid lifelessly to the bottom.

"Holy shit!" he remembered saying as his pulse raced from the coursing adrenaline.

"Shh!" Peter's hand went across Mike's mouth. "Where are you supposed to be right now?"

"The bathroom," he answered as Peter removed his hand.

"Go. Now. Then get back to class."

"What about—?"

"Never mind. Just go."

Mike watched from the top of the stairs as Peter walked down toward the body. He knelt down while pulling his right hand into his sleeve, and then reached for Max's shoelaces. With a tug, the laces came untied and Peter quickly turned around and ran back to the top of the stairs.

"What are you waiting for?" Peter asked.

"I didn't know what you were doing."

"I was covering your ass. Now go. Meet me after school."

Before the bell rang, signaling the end of the day, an announcement was made over the loud speaker for the students to remain in their seats after the bell. They made no mention of Max's death, only reported there was an accident and police were on the scene.

Overwhelming panic encompassed Mike. The torture his mind played out during those fifteen minutes had been far worse than the actual interrogation. He and Peter were questioned for the same reasons; both were out of class during the possible time of death and for the fight that morning Max's friends reported.

Unable to speak with Peter before the interrogation, Mike was a shaky mess afraid of saying the wrong thing, but he did the one thing he knew best and played dumb. The death was ruled an accident, not a single adult could believe the boy had been murdered by one of his peers, and their partnership was born.

Before meeting Peter, Mike could not remember a time when he wasn't afraid. Loneliness and Fear, the two dominant emotions that defined his childhood, but Peter came along and taught him how to stand-up for himself, to kill, to be cool.

Mike smiled as a glimpse of all their victims over the years flashed before his mind's eye, from their start with woodland creatures and neighborhood pets to Julie-The-Coffee-Bitch two weeks ago. *Good times*, he thought as he opened a cupboard and retrieved a glass. Once the glass was filled from the tap, he turned around and swigged a mouthful of water, swishing it back and forth across his dry tongue.

Peter's up, he thought, seeing a light illuminating the shadows from under the basement door.

"Damnit!" Peter exclaimed as he fumbled with the collection of wires. *This is more hassle than it's worth*, he thought as he dragged himself out from underneath the large, oak work bench. *But who else could do it right?*

He knew the answer. No one.

He took a moment to gaze upon the six computer monitors he had lined up—one for each server he and Mike scattered across Florida. They would allow him to monitor their activity and act as a safety net should his faith in his skills be misguided. With the proxy to mask their activity in place, the dummy servers to bounce the signal, and the static IP address he purchased, the forum would be virtually invisible. In theory.

The wires dangling through the hole he'd cut into the work surface and branching this way and that boiled his blood. It was chaos.

"I need some more twist-ties," Peter mumbled.

He walked past the basement stairs and over to Mike's work bench. Upon the shelves mounted over the work surface identical to Peter's were numerous glass jars housing a variety of useful consumables: nails, screws, paper clips, elastics. Anything you'd want or need could be found, even things that would never cross his mind such as marbles and buttons.

Peter sorted through the assortment of wire ties and selected five, short, black ones to blend in with the wires, then returned to his setup.

The plan was to get the network up and running and to create a subnet mask. Then store all the information for the website on Google servers. He alone would decide its members via e-vites and cryptic messages on other web sites and message boards. Any smart enough to decode his genius deserved to be a member, and should any law enforcement agents discover the site, they would be led on one wild goose chase.

The basement door opened and Mike descended the creaky steps with a glass of water in his hand.

"What are you doing up?" Peter asked, not bothering to turn away from the computer monitors.

"Needed a drink. What about you?"

"Couldn't sleep."

"How much longer?"

"Man," Peter said, dragging the word, "you're impatient."

"Noooo," he said, mocking Peter, "just anxious to help others."

A chuckle escaped Peter's lips. Life was his to take from

whomever he desired and helping others contradicted his beliefs, but Mike was his best friend, a brother, had been for years, and there was nothing he wouldn't do for him. Even if it meant suppressing his true self.

"What's so funny?" Mike asked as he squatted to see Peter.

"I just find it odd, that's all."

"What? That we're going to be helping people rather than slaughtering them."

Peter shook his head. "You just want to see their pictures."

Mike blushed. "These are more than people, they're—"

"Don't say it!" Peter tied off the last disorderly cable and slid out from underneath the work bench. "For the love of God, don't say it."

A small smile formed on Mike's face and Peter realized he was only doing it now to rile him. "Brothers in Blood!"

Bastard, he thought and smiled as well.

"You done?"

"Not quite," Peter said, pulling his high-back chair in close. "I still have to design the forum and encrypt it."

"Anything I can do?"

"You could leave. That would be a great help."

"It's not so far-fetched for me to want to help others... you know...like you helped me."

"Call it a lapse in judgment."

Mike crossed his arms in front of his chest. "C'mon, there's gotta be something I can do?"

"Actually." Peter paused. "Why don't you go troll some of your gore sites and find us some worthy members."

"Now that's something I *can* do," Mike said with a wide grin.

<First Communion>
Marsheila Rockwell

"Forgive me, Father, for I have sinned," intoned the man the press had dubbed 'the Communion Killer.' The ritual words slipped out of his mouth along with a thin stream of drool that made Father McKeirnan shudder in disgust and look away quickly. The old priest secretly viewed this once-a-month visit to the Montana Institute of Mental Health (what the locals affectionately called the Asylum) as penance for sins of his youth that he could no longer remember, but which must have been particularly vile to warrant this duty. Thank God it would be the last such trip; Steve Pederson's lawyers had finally lost their long battle to keep him out of prison. He had been sentenced to death, and would be taken to the State Penitentiary in Deer Lodge just as soon as his session with Father McKeirnan was over.

Pederson struggled briefly but was unable to cross himself, bound as he was in a stained strait-jacket that looked as if it hadn't been removed since he'd been committed, nearly a year ago. Father McKeirnan mused that it might not have been—given the brutal way in which this man had slain his victims, he was probably lucky they hadn't gagged him.

The Communion Killer subsided with a frustrated grunt and began what was, by now, a familiar litany to them both.

"I was seven years old when I broke the fifth commandment for the first time...."

Stevie's grandmother cinched the white tie a little too tightly, then stood back to admire her handiwork. Stevie straightened his back before she could tell him to and stared at the hand-carved wooden rosary clutched in one of her parchment-like claws. His First Confession was to be this Thursday, followed by his First Communion on Saturday, and his grandmother was certain he was going to screw it up, so they were conducting a full dress rehearsal. Again. While all the other kids in his CCD class were at the parish hall, scarfing down pizza and soda as a reward for two years of hard work. But Stevie didn't dare complain—Grandma used a wooden ruler just as effectively as any of the nuns at school, in places and ways those waddling penguins would never dare, and that was just one of the weapons in her repertoire. His stiff spine and downcast eyes weren't enough to please her, though.

"Steven Pederson! Those shoes are scuffed! Is that how you show respect for Our Lord? By preparing to partake of *Him* looking like some beggar off the street?" The old woman's querulous voice rose to a screech that neatly camouflaged the sound of the electrical cord swinging through the air.

Stevie was utterly unprepared for the stinging blow that caught him just below the hip. Even through the tough polyester of his hand-me-down suit, he knew he'd have a welt that would last for days.

He imprisoned his cry of pain behind quickly clenched teeth before it could escape—such a display of weakness would only provoke Grandma further.

Stevie's grandmother shifted the cord—Stevie recognized it as the one to her electric teapot—to the same hand that held her rosary. Then she stepped forward more quickly than a woman her age should have been able to and grabbed a handful of his thick blond hair. She jerked his head up, hard.

"What is the Holy Eucharist, boy?" she demanded, her watery blue eyes boring into his own.

"The Body, Blood, Soul and Divinity of Our Lord Jesus Christ, under the appearance of bread and wine," Stevie recited dutifully, wincing when her hand twitched toward him, setting the rosary beads to clacking.

"And John 6:56 and 57?" She slapped the cord and rosary, now tangled together, against her leg, waiting for him to stumble.

Stevie thought quickly, his eyes darting from the cord to his grandmother's too-large pupils, and back again. "He who eats my flesh and drinks my blood abides in me, and I in him," he finally spit out, just as her arm began to rise again. "As the living Father sent me, and I live because of the Father, so he who eats me will live because of me."

"So when you receive Holy Communion…" Grandma trailed off dangerously, but Stevie felt a rush of relief at the prompt; he knew this one.

"We receive Jesus. All good Catholics have Jesus inside them." It was the right answer; his grandmother said it often enough herself.

But for some reason, this time the response only seemed to infuriate the old woman further. She brought her arm up and down again in one quick stroke, and the electrical cord sliced across Stevie's unprotected face. As his hand flew to the trail of fire along his left cheek and encountered a wetness he realized must be blood, his grandmother railed at him.

"That's just the problem, boy! You're *not* a good Catholic…no one who prepares so poorly for his First Holy Communion could be! You're weak, and you're going to Hell, just as surely as your slut of a mother and that heathen who fathered you!"

She punctuated every sentence with another blow from the cord, until his arms and face were covered in bloody welts and scratches from the rosary beads, made even more painful by salt from the tears that coursed openly down his cheeks.

"I'm sorry, Grandma, I'm sorry," he cried, falling to his knees. "I'll be good, I'll be a good Catholic, I won't be like them, please just stop, Grandma, please, I promise…."

Stevie's grandmother continued to rain blows down on his head and shoulder, too gone in her fury to pay any heed to his pleading. One blow landed across the palm of his outstretched hand, and his fingers closed around the cord reflexively. Before he could stop to think, Stevie reached out with his other hand, grabbed the cord, and pulled.

His grandmother, caught off guard, stumbled and fell heavily, landing on the stark wooden floor she was too cheap to have carpeted, no matter how cold it got in the winter. She took the full force of the fall on her right hip, and Stevie heard a cracking noise just before his grandmother began to scream, this time in pain.

"Ahhhhh, my hip! Oh, Stevie, I think it's broken! Help me!" She reached out toward him as if in supplication, agony etched clearly across her thin and wrinkled face.

Stevie climbed unsteadily to his feet and moved to stand over his grandmother, the rosary clattering to the floor as he switched the electrical cord to his right hand. His stronger hand.

"Stevie?"

At the fearful tone, Stevie felt a surge of emotion so powerful, he began to sweat and shake. It took him a moment to identify the feeling—pure, unadulterated rage. He laughed suddenly, emboldened by the helplessness that radiated from his always so-formidable grandmother.

"Who's the weak one now, Grandma?" he asked softly when the short-lived laughter subsided. With a smile, he whipped the cord down through the air with all the force his seven-year-old frame could muster. The sound of the rubber-encased lash impacting against brittle flesh filled his ears again and again, drowning out the old woman's cries as they became whimpers, and then slowly ceased.

"I don't know how long I beat her, but she looked like Christ scourged at the pillar before I finally stopped. Then I went upstairs and took a bath, changed into jeans and a long-sleeved T-shirt, and came back downstairs. I started a fire in the fireplace—something Grandma would never let me do unless it was below zero outside—and turned the oven on in the kitchen. I'd seen someone do it on a TV movie, so I figured it would work. Then I left for the party at the church. I was four blocks away when the house blew, and nobody ever knew Grandma was dead before the flames reached her.

"So I didn't get to go through either my First Confession or Communion with my CCD class; instead they put me in a foster home while they tried to sort out who would take custody of me. The family I ended up with wasn't Catholic, so didn't see the need to take me, and it was years before I was finally able to receive that sacrament. Then, when I tried to confess what I'd done to the priest, he told me I was just experiencing 'survivor's guilt' and that I should go see a counselor. He said as long as I was truly sorry for whatever role I might have accidentally played in my grandmother's death, the Lord would forgive me."

Pederson leaned forward to regard Father McKeirnan with an intense look. "But I wasn't sorry. I was *glad*." When the old priest didn't respond, Pederson sat back on the cot. "So I was never absolved of her death, and never able to receive the Holy Eucharist, but that didn't stop me. I found another way."

Pederson continued his list of sins, relentlessly detailing the murders that came after. The majority of his victims were old women who he picked up on their way home from daily Mass, but he killed men and children as well—all Catholics that had recently received Communion.

Despite the horrific nature of the crimes, only some of which had ever been discovered, Father McKeirnan had heard the list so many times, and Pederson's tone was so monotonous, that the old priest found himself drifting off. On some level, he couldn't stand to pay too much attention to the particulars—in his almost twenty-five years as a priest, Father McKeirnan had never had to deal with a murderer, let alone a serial killer as depraved as Pederson. Neither had the State of Montana. The fact that Pederson was a patient here at MIMH, instead of an inmate in Deer Lodge, was a testament to the system's inexperience with such vile creatures—and to the craftiness of Pederson's lawyers.

As Pederson droned on, Father McKeirnan found himself being lulled into a dream state, where he could easily envision the atrocities Pederson described....

"The Mass is ended. Go in peace."

"Thanks be to God," Steve murmured, along with the ten or so other people who had braved the rain to go to the six a.m. service. He'd drifted into town less than a month ago and had been attending daily Mass at St. Cecilia's ever since, though he never received Communion. He couldn't; the stain of mortal sin on his soul was still too fresh, even after sixteen years.

As he rose from his pew to leave, he noticed an old woman—Mrs. Garrett, he'd heard the priest call her—struggling with the kneeler across from him. After genuflecting quickly, he crossed the aisle and bent to help her. The heavy wood rose easily.

Mrs. Garrett smiled up at him gratefully, the expression softening her wrinkles and giving a glimpse of how beautiful she must have been once. Steve just nodded and continued back to the narthex, where he crossed himself with holy water and turned up his collar, getting ready for the dash to his car.

"Ah, I'd hoped the rain would have let up by now," a cracked voice said in his ear, and Steve turned to see Mrs. Garrett pulling on a long raincoat. It was then that he noticed the galoshes she wore, still muddy from her trek to the church a half hour earlier.

Steve smiled sympathetically at the old woman, admiring her dedication. He wouldn't have come today if he didn't have a car. Mrs. Garrett was a devout woman—a good Catholic. Like his grandma had been.

"Can I give you a lift home, Mrs. Garrett?" he asked, offering an arm.

The wrinkles softened again. "Thank you, son. That would be wonderful."

The rain hammered Steve's 1980 Manza fiercely, as if trying to beat its way through the metal roof to the soft, vulnerable flesh housed within. Traffic lights were a smear of color in the pervading grey, and Steve nearly drove past Mrs. Garrett's house before spotting the address painted on the curb, its numbers half-obscured by storm water racing down the gutter to be swallowed by the nearest greedy catch basin.

Steve maneuvered the car as close to the curb as he could get and stepped out into the downpour. In the few seconds it took to open his umbrella and duck beneath it, his hair was soaked. He wiped water out of his face with one hand as he waded around to the other door to help Mrs. Garrett out.

Huddling together, they slogged through wide puddles and mud up the cracked sidewalk to a small porch. Once there, Steve shook out his umbrella and ran a hand through his sodden hair.

"It's not fit weather for driving. Why don't you come

in for some cocoa and sandwiches and wait for it to die down a bit?"

Steve looked out toward his car, a bluish smudge barely distinguishable from the monochrome gloom of rain and pavement. He looked back at Mrs. Garrett in her bright yellow raincoat, who was unlocking her front door with a key she had retrieved from beneath the welcome mat. As she bent forward to replace the key, a wooden rosary slipped from her pocket and landed with a muted clatter of beads on the mat. Steve swooped down to retrieve the beads and replace them in Mrs. Garrett's outstretched hand. As his fingers brushed against the parchment-like skin of her palm, Steve felt a jolt of adrenalin course through him. That decided him.

"I guess it wouldn't hurt. I *am* a little hungry."

Mrs. Garrett smiled, tucking the rosary back into her pocket after kissing the crucifix reverently. "Good boy."

After removing her coat and galoshes in the foyer and instructing him where to hang his own jacket and umbrella, Mrs. Garrett led him through dim hallways to the back of her small home. The house was cold, and smelled of dust, dead flowers and stale cat urine. Pictures lined the walls and fought old books and figurines for space on the many shelves. Most were black and white or sepia-toned, depicting unsmiling men and women in clothing from another era. Here and there, a color photo would stand out against the faded wallpaper and book covers, depicting impish children captured in a fleeting moment of stillness.

Steve's sneakers squeaked against the hardwood floors as they crossed in front of a fireplace, long unused and probably unusable. Twin pictures of the Sacred and Immaculate Hearts beamed kindly at him as he passed.

The kitchen was a stark contrast to the rest of the house. Bright copper pans hung from a low ceiling, watercolors and magnets in the shapes of states covered the old refrigerator, and fragrant herbs grew in neat boxes along the windowsills. Steve nearly stumbled when a furry something darted past his feet to twine itself about Mrs. Garrett's legs while she laughed delightedly.

"Francis, don't be rude. Say hello to our guest," she scolded the brown cat, bending down to pat the animal affectionately as another cat, this one a striking white, bounded up to her. "You, too, Dominic."

"Nice names," Steve commented as he sat at the kitchen table where she'd pulled out a chair for him moments before. The long tablecloth, adorned with pink and yellow roses, brushed the laces of his shoes.

"I always hoped one of my boys would take to the religious life," Mrs. Garret replied as she shooed the cats away and began heating water in a teapot—not an electric one, Steve was unaccountably glad to see. "But they fell away from the Church despite my efforts, though they do come 'round for Midnight Mass and the Easter Vigil, even receive Communion on those days, though I suspect perhaps they oughtn't."

She turned a sharp eye toward Steve. "And you. I've been watching you. Every day you come to Mass, but you never receive Our Lord. Why is that?"

Steve waited so long to answer that she finally turned away and began fixing the sandwiches, cutting a block of cheddar into thick slices with a sharp knife before moving on to carve ruddy beefsteak tomatoes into fat sections. Her hands shook slightly with age.

"Whoever, therefore, eats the bread and drinks the cup of the Lord in an unworthy manner will be guilty of profaning the body and blood of the Lord," Steve said softly, quoting the eleventh chapter of First Corinthians, his words heavy with emotion.

"Nonsense," the old woman replied with alacrity, rounding on him and unconsciously brandishing the knife.

"That sounds like an excuse one of my boys would use. If there's something keeping you from the Eucharist, then go to Confession. Father Johnson offers Reconciliation every morning before Mass."

Steve regarded her steadily for a moment before replying. "I can't be absolved if I'm not truly repentant for what I did, Mrs. Garrett."

Mrs. Garrett blinked several times, nonplussed by his response. Unable to formulate a reply, she returned to slicing tomatoes, her grip decidedly more unsteady.

Steve rose quietly from his chair and moved to stand behind her, watching the up and down motion of hands that reminded him, suddenly and unpleasantly, of his grandmother's always angry claws.

"Let me help you," he said, reaching out to grasp the knife. Mrs. Garrett jerked away instinctively, startled by his nearness, and the finely honed blade sliced cleanly through the first joint on her left index finger.

For the space of several erratic heartbeats, they both stared at the severed digit and the blood that pooled on the cutting board to mix obscenely with the watery juice and seeds from the tomatoes.

Without conscious thought, Steve crossed himself quickly, murmured, "The Body of Christ," and picked up the end of Mrs. Garrett's finger, swallowing it whole, blood, bone, nail and all.

Mrs. Garrett watched in horror, transfixed by the sight. Her mouth opened and closed repeatedly, and a piteous string of half-moans, half-whimpers escaped from between her suddenly chattering teeth.

Steve took the hand towel from the oven door and wrapped what was left of Mrs. Garrett's still-bleeding finger gently in its soft confines, pausing for a brief moment to admire how the bright crimson stain blossomed against the white cloth to match the yellow and pink roses already there.

He led her over to the table and made her sit. Sitting down opposite her, he grasped her injured hand and squeezed, too tightly, eliciting a guttural noise from the terrified woman. He chided her gently. "Those who receive Our Lord in the hand must take care not to allow any particles to fall or be scattered, and any that are must be consumed just as the Host proper is consumed, for He is present in every atom." At her confused look, he continued. "You received Our Lord less than twenty minutes ago. Jesus is still inside you, just as He is inside all good Catholics who receive Communion in a state of grace. He abides in you, Mrs. Garrett, His flesh and blood becoming part of your flesh and blood through the process of digestion. I could no more leave a piece of you uneaten than I could a particle of the Host."

Pain, blood loss and shock combined to overwhelm the old woman's faculties at last, and with a groan that was almost grateful, her eyes rolled back in her head and she slumped, unconscious, in her seat.

Steve returned to the counter and retrieved the knife, his twisted theological discourse uninterrupted. "And just as no Catholic worth the name would ignore the bulk of the host in favor of consuming just a particle, I must finish the Paschal Banquet He has so generously set before me."

Kneeling over Mrs. Garrett's body, he murmured, "*Domine non sum dignus*," and plunged the knife repeatedly into her chest until he was sure she was dead. Only then, when he was covered from head to toe in her holy blood, did he begin to feast.

When the list of offenses was finally complete, nearly an hour later, and Father McKeirnan had explained, once again, how Pederson's actions and beliefs were heinous distortions of actual Catholic doctrine, quiet descended to fill the small room.

Into the silence, he asked the question he'd asked Pederson so many times before, only to be both saddened and sickened by the response.

"And do you repent of the sins confessed here today, which have offended God and are worthy only of His just punishment?"

And to Father McKeirnan's great surprise, Pederson answered in a voice thick with unshed tears. "Yes, Father. I do."

Father McKeirnan hesitated only a moment before completing the ritual—if Pederson were not truly repentant, God would know, and there would be no absolution granted, despite his utterance of the sacred words. But Pederson was on his way to the gas chamber, and men as bad as or worse than the Communion Killer had come to their senses in those last precious hours of life. Who was he to question what graces God might grant a man at such a time?

"...may God give you pardon and peace, and I absolve you in the name of the Father, and of the Son, and of the Holy Spirit. Amen."

"Amen," Pederson replied, still unable to cross himself, but with a smile on his face that could only be described as beatific.

As Father McKeirnan sat back in his metal chair to regard the young man before him, Pederson leaned forward with a look so earnest it reminded the old priest of a puppy, eager to please his master and be praised.

"Father, have you had Communion today?"

Father McKeirnan frowned. Considering Pederson's background, that was not an auspicious question.

"Yes. Priests are required to say Mass at least once a day, whether in private or for a congregation."

Pederson's smile widened, and his eyes shone. "Do you think, Father, that I could receive Communion today, for the first and last time?"

Surprised for the second time in as many minutes, Father McKeirnan considered the request. Although he brought a small supply of both consecrated wine and Communion wafers with him every time he visited Pederson, he'd never had cause to actually use them. But Pederson, he had to believe, with the help of God's grace, had truly repented of his crimes and was asking for viaticum, the Holy Eucharist received as the last sacrament for those whose journey of faith in this life was about to end. He could not, in good conscience, refuse the request.

"Very well."

He made the preparations quickly; a glance at his watch revealed that the guards would be coming to take Pederson away in less than half an hour. Hurrying through the rite, he approached Pederson, who stood to receive, tongue extended.

"The Body of Christ," he murmured, and lifted the consecrated host in one hand.

But the thought of coming into contact with Pederson's copious drool was just too repellant, and instead of placing the wafer on the man's tongue, he held it a hair's breadth above and let it drop.

Pederson, too eager, pulled his tongue in at the same time and the host bounced off his teeth and fell to the floor before either priest or prisoner could react.

Pederson looked down at the wafer, now cracked in half on the hard concrete, then back up at the priest, disappointment and fury warring across his visage.

The anger won out, and Father McKeirnan registered the change too late. Before he could step back, Pederson reared his head back and then slammed his forehead into Father McKeirnan's face, breaking the old priest's nose and sending him sprawling to the floor. In seconds, Pederson was atop him, holding the old man down with his own body weight while his teeth tore at the priest's unprotected throat.

Over his own screams and the rush of blood in his ears, Father McKeirnan could hear Pederson mumbling around mouthfuls of skin and stringy muscle.

"At last…I don't need the host now that I have you, Father, acting *in persona Christi*…he who eats my flesh and drinks my blood has eternal life…*your* flesh and *your* blood, Father…*my* First Communion…."

\<scratching the itch\>
Keith Gouveia

"For someone who was against it, Peter sure has embraced this community," Mike said as he perused the gallery of images his partner had uploaded to the forum—a variable slide show of all their transgressions.

Mike was also surprised to find Peter's participation with the forum didn't stop there. Beneath his tag name—silens iuguolo—was a number which correlated to over a hundred and fifty posts.

"It hasn't even been a month," Mike mumbled before clicking the digital display.

The hyperlink took him to a page listing all the topics Peter had either engaged in or started.

Son-of-a-bitch, he thought, surprised by the brief display of Peter's actions.

The first line of every post was listed under the topic header. His sarcastic, introverted partner had given disposal tips to Harbinger51; weapon cleaning dos and don'ts to Playdead; dating advice to S1ngledad; church etiquette to Godshand, and puppy training tips to Gothslayer. Adding insult to injury, he had done so in a polite, charming manner.

"What are you doing?"

Mike's hand quickly slid the mouse so that the cursor hovered over the exit icon, but he knew he was already busted.

"You're spying on me, don't try to deny it."

He turned around to find Peter standing with his arms crossed and lips pursed.

"I didn't expect you home so soon." He cracked a smile.

Peter's arms relaxed and fell to his sides. "Not that you would know, but we closed early. All my pieces sold."

"Excellent."

"Don't change the subject." Peter placed his hands down on the armrests of Mike's chair and leaned in. "Why are you spying on me?"

"I wasn't *spying*—"

"Bullshit!"

"All right. Jeez! I was just curious to know if you liked the site. God!"

Peter narrowed his eyes and after a long pause, straightened his back. "You could have just asked."

"I was sitting here bored."

"You should have come to the gallery."

Mike waved his hand, dismissing the notion. "Carol gives me the creeps. We should have offed her years ago."

"She's too good at her job. Look around…none of this would be possible without her, and you know it."

"Whatever." Mike swiveled his chair back around to face the monitor. "So what's with this fancy handle. You showing off your superior intellect again?"

Peter released a nasal sigh and Mike could only assume he rolled his eyes as well, but he did not argue the point.

"What does that even mean?" Mike pestered.

"It's latin for silent killer."

With his lips together and his shoulders straight, Mike mocked Peter and repeated his answer in the quiet sanctity of his mind.

"I saw that," said Peter.

Mike smiled. "Just a little harmless ball busting between friends."

"Speaking of busting balls, I've found us a new playmate."

"At your art gallery?" Mike swiveled around once more. "What did he do?"

"Why do you have to assume it's a guy?"

Mike cocked his head to the side. "That's a…what do you call it…rhetorical, right?"

"I suppose. Anyway. This guy was a total dick to one of the waitresses. I watched him hit on her all night, each of his advancements shot down." Peter's arms articulated every word. "Finally, he out right accuses her of being a lesbian, loud enough for the entire gallery to hear."

"Again?" Mike asked. "If we start killing everyone who's rude to a server, they're going to label us the Service Industry Avenger!"

"Bullying is bullying!"

Mike nodded and asked, "What did she do?"

"What could she do? She ran in the bathroom and didn't come out until the doors were closed."

"You followed him home?"

Peter returned the sideways glance Mike had given him just moments before. "Guy lives in Wickham Park."

"Really," Mike said, "Fancy. Could be tough though."

Peter scrunched his face. "Nah. Those townhomes were built well with an eight-inch concrete wall between units for soundproofing."

"I don't like it when you're too confident."

"Relax." Peter patted Mike's shoulder, then said, "We've got this. It's late. He went home alone. No sweat."

"All right. I'll get the gear."

At nearly one a.m., the streets of Windermere were deserted and dark as pitch with not a single house light on.

Upon seeing the manicured community, Mike was instantly jealous. The housing units consisted of five homes, each center unit had two gabled windows and was a darker shade of brown then the other four to accentuate the structure and provide a focal point. The front doors had their own small porch roof, perfectly shaped, knee-high bushes and solar lights rimmed the walk ways, the oak trees full and Mike could only imagine the ample shade they provided from the Florida sun, and the grass held a vibrant green color.

He turned to Peter and asked, "Why can't we live here?"

"Everyone knows everyone's business. Trust me. We're better off far away from any subdivision or complex."

"I suppose," Mike replied, turning back to look out the passenger's side window.

Peter cut the headlights as he made a left-hand turn. Behind the townhomes ran alleyways that hooked into the main road—perfect for avoiding any night owls. With the engine killed, the car rolled silently toward the desired driveway.

Before exiting the car, Peter pointed at the door they wanted. The target lived in the second unit from the left. Mike nodded, then followed his partner's lead.

Once at the door, Peter crouched down—already holding his torsion wrench and his hook-shaped pick. With both tips inserted into the keyhole, he worked the mechanism as if he were Houdini reincarnated and no matter how many times he saw it, Mike was always amazed. One by one, the tumblers gave way, and then Peter used the torsion wrench to turn the plug. The lock disengaged with a muffled *click*. Slowly, Peter cracked the door and found resistance from a deadbolt chain. Without skipping a beat or getting upset, he pulled the door back just enough to let slack in the chain and squeeze his lock pick into the space.

With a steady hand, Peter slid the chain across its housing and it fell away. He was careful to not allow it to hit the door and chime a warning. The door swung open silently, and they were greeted by darkness.

"Mind your step," Peter whispered as he entered.

Mike wanted to tell him it wasn't his first time at the dance, but thought better of it. Peter would only hold his tongue for so long and verbally assault him once they were home.

The layout of the townhome was standard, a living area, bathroom, and kitchen on the first floor and two bedrooms and a second bathroom upstairs. Fine art decorated the walls, but Mike did not recognize any of the pieces.

He tapped Peter on the shoulder, causing him to turn around. "Any of these worth anything?" he asked.

Peter released a nasal sigh. "We're not thieves."

He shrugged his shoulders as Peter turned back around.

As they ascended the stairs, Mike realized how cramped he and Peter would be in such an abode and the desire to move to the location faded from his mind.

They found their latest victim already in bed, fully clothed and laying on his back with his right foot planted against the floor.

The room must have been spinning on him, Mike thought, then wondered just how much of the free champagne the man had sampled at the gallery.

"No challenge in this," Peter whispered.

"Do you want to call it off?" he asked in a similar octave.

Peter shook his head, then pulled the nearly half-inch wide cable ties from his pocket.

Mike stood at the ready, his leg bouncing at the knee. *Been too long*, he thought.

Without waking the man, Peter bound his wrists to the headboard and then secured his feet.

The man's eyes fluttered open as Peter moved into position to gag him. Mike was ready and quickly slammed his right hand over the man's mouth and nose. He struggled, but soon realized just how fucked he was.

"Hello asshole," Peter said, getting right in the man's face and allowing him to see his attacker.

Eyes wide with tears threatening to run, the man mumbled incoherently. Mike assumed he was pleading for his life, but his hand remained locked in place until Peter said otherwise.

"You've got something to say?" Peter often toyed with his prey like a cat playfully batting a mouse with its paw before tearing into it.

"Mmhmm," the man uttered as he nodded.

Peter gave Mike the look, and with his free hand, Mike removed the nine-inch long blade tucked behind him and showed it to the man.

"If you scream for help," Peter said, "we will kill you, and all your neighbors, before the cops can get through the gate. Understand?"

"Mmhmm."

With the blade pressed against the man's Adam's apple, Mike removed his hand.

"Please don't kill me. Take whatever you want…there's a fake wall panel in my closet."

Peter reached over the man and grabbed the knife. "Check it out."

Surprised by the demand, Mike stood in place for a moment wondering if he was truly contemplating the offer.

Peter cocked his head to the right and widened his eyes.

Yep. He's serious.

Without complaint, Mike turned away from the bed and walked toward the bi-fold closet door. After opening it, he pushed the hanging clothes aside.

"Well?" Peter asked.

"Hold on," Mike replied.

"Turn the light on," said the man strapped to the bed, voice trembling with fear. "The cord should be in front of you."

"Ah!" Mike pulled the chain link and the fluorescent light pushed away the shadows to reveal a narrow notch. Wedging his fingers into it, he popped the panel free. "What the…!"

Stacked atop on another were three rows of VCR tapes, each labeled with a woman's name.

"What is it?" Peter asked.

Mike cracked a smile. "Someone's been busy."

"Never mind those," said the man as he struggled against his bonds. "The money's in the safe. Right there. Take it and go!"

Peter removed the blades edge from the man's throat and walked over. He stood beside Mike, staring down at the stash of what Mike assumed to be sex tapes.

"What are you thinkin' partner?" he asked the quiet Peter. "Should we open the safe?"

"No," he said, then turned back toward the man. "We're not thieves, but these tapes have given me a deliciously wicked idea."

"Oh yeah. What is it?"

Peter turned to him with a devilish grin. "Feel like getting your hands dirty?"

"Do you have to ask?" Mike answered.

We're live at Wickham Park where a man has been brutally slain in what appears to be a crime of passion. Police received a phone call from the victim's cell phone, presumably from the murderer, alerting them to the heinous act of violence one can only describe as cruel and unusual.

When they arrived, the police found Jonathon Dupere strapped to his bed, naked and covered in his own blood. His testicles snipped off and rammed down his throat. Scattered across the floor, broken and unwound, police documented over fifty sex tapes. Somewhere in the mess of smut they believe they'll find their suspect. Police also report that the body had been desecrated, but refused to get into specifics at this time.

We'll bring further details as we get them. Until then, this is Maria Santiago for Channel Nine News. Back to you, Tony.

<The Calling>
Giovanna Lagana

The deer came out of nowhere onto the road. In reflex, Frank Peters turned the steering wheel to the right to avoid hitting it and nearly swerved into the deep ditch.

"Shit!" he shouted as he regained control of the car while gazing into his side mirror. He could see the dumb animal just stood still, staring at the vehicle's departure with wide, shocked eyes.

"That's the most excitement I've had today," he said to himself as his drumming heartbeat slowed to normal and he wiped his clammy hand on his blue jeans. "Damn, and I thought this day would have been different."

Frank had sensed it in his bones when he woke up that morning that something big was going to happen today. He craved it and the adrenaline rush that came with the calling, the addictive elixir that put him on a high he hated to come down from. And having not been on that high for the past four months had him feeling numb. He went about his daily routine, but his mind and soul hardly participated in the monotonous activities.

Instead, he daydreamed of the past and wished he could relive it. Too much time had passed, though. Maybe it ended and they forgot to tell him about it. After all, he was just their conduit. Their means to an end. Now, they probably didn't need him anymore.

The feeling this morning made him sure they'd be calling him again, but the day was almost over and silence still hovered over him like a dark cloud raining on his parade. *Oh, well. They obviously don't need me anymore*, he thought.

Rubbing his tense neck, he stared at the horizon up ahead. When his stomach made a growling noise, he realized he hadn't eaten anything all day. He wasn't up to going to a greasy hamburger joint to eat. Right now, he needed tranquility. Idle town folks' chitchat bored him. And for some reason, they all wanted to talk to him in every town he stopped. Did he look like he cared a shit about who they were, what they did, or what they liked? Hell no. Just once he wished they'd leave him alone so he could eat in peace, then be on his way.

A peanut butter and jam sandwich with some chips and a Coke should stop his hunger pangs for a bit. Once nighttime rolled around, the chatty folks would head home and the loners would come out to eat and play. Then he'd find a diner to have a scrumptious, juicy burger and beer to satisfy his hunger without having to entertain the cheery, snoopy town people.

Parking his trailer onto a side dirt road that led to nothing but the woods to the right, he headed for the kitchenette to get his grub. The bread was stale and the peanut butter oily because of the heat, but he ate the sandwich he made with little more than a grimace.

The barbeque chips and the Coke thankfully washed away the bad taste in his mouth afterward while he stood staring out the window. When the barren view bored him, he turned to look at the glass and oak display case he had on the wall to his right. In the stand, forty-four cells phones were aligned in eight rows of five and one of four. Their colorful fronts and tiny keypads caught his attention. He had them in chronological order of course. That was the only way to store them for sentimental reasons.

Looking at his first phone, the Blackberry 8700, he remembered the day he got it. He knew nothing about cell phones or Smart-phones back then. They really didn't interest him, but the moment he got this one, things changed. His curiosity urged him to learn everything about them from the inside out, even their circuit boards and complex microprocessors.

Gazing at the incomplete display now, irked him. He was missing one more cell phone to make the display casing complete. As it stood, it looked gauche. He was hoping he'd get another phone today so that he could add to the collection, but it looked as though his inkling was wrong.

Burping, he wiped his mouth with the back of his hand and headed to the driver's seat. Time to head out of no man's land and back on the road.

Even if the day turned out to be like all the others, being on the move still had him hopeful. Maybe something interesting would cross his path and entertain him for a bit.

Two hours passed. The sun began to set and the full moon would rise soon. All Frank had seen was the open, empty road with a few passing cars. Nothing else.

His hunger had come back and he decided to get off at the next exit to find a place to eat. When he came within sight of a cell phone tower, a ringing sound began to chime in his ear. It started out as a low hum, but increased in frequency until he had to shake his head to ease the pain in his eardrums.

"Hell, yes," he cheered waiting for what came next.

He parked to the side of the road. Thankfully, it meant his bones had been right. Tonight, he'd get a serving of his addictive elixir once again.

When the Callers' voices followed the high frequency sound, his mouth broke into a smile.

Frank..., they chimed loudly in unison.

"Yes?" His voice cracked. His excitement getting the better of him, it seemed.

You must bring us one more.

"Just show me the way." He nodded while staring at the high tower nearby.

Just then, a car passed him on the road doing about 80 miles an hour. He glanced at it in reflex for a second, then returned his attention to his right.

That one, the Callers responded in a calming tone after another minute elapsed.

With his hand on the clutch, he put the vehicle into drive and headed on his mission without uttering another word. He didn't need to. His focus clear, he put his plan in motion. And damn, he'd enjoy every second of it.

It didn't take him long to meet up with the red, speeding Lexus that passed him a few minutes ago. Although he couldn't register much detail of the car because the descending sun's rays were too dim to illuminate the interior of the vehicle, he could make out the driver was alone. *Sweet!*

He kept three cars' distance away from it and just followed in silence while his mind wandered. He curiously wondered about the driver. Was it a woman or a man? A business person or an artist? Whoever it was, they had done something bad, real bad and now the Callers wanted him to deliver their justice. He couldn't have been more delighted, for thanks to those Callers, he had seen ecstasy firsthand and nothing on earth could match it.

The look of utter terror his victims displayed the moment they knew Death came a knocking and they were crossing the threshold to the other side was priceless. A shiver crawled up his spine with images of his past victims. Oh, the visions of blood vessels forming, spreading, and busting in the whites of their eyes while he slowly chocked the air out of them was like fireworks on the Fourth of July for him.

It made his veins and arteries excited and his blood

surged through them with an unrelenting vigor. That was his addictive elixir, for at the moment his victim's saw their deaths was the moment he felt the most alive. It was as if their life energy seeped out of their sweating pores and absorbed into his skin melding with his life source.

Perhaps it was the Callers doing, the melding. Maybe they channeled the victim's life force and fused it to his. Who knew? But thanks to them, he knew what Heaven on Earth felt like. Or in the Biblical view, Hell on Earth. *Yeah, baby.*

When the Lexus got off on the next exit and his victim drove to a secluded street ten minutes later, Frank's heart began to pump blood fast through his body with anticipation. He slowed down, parked a little farther ahead, and made sure a huge bush hid him when he came out to spy.

As the sinner opened the garage door with a remote control, he lost his breath. A motion sensor light came on, illuminating the driveway his victim parked in. When his target opened the door, he realized it was a female. He frowned. He kind of hoped for a male. Given their stamina, they put up more of a physical fight than his female victims had, thus making his addictive elixir last longer.

But he couldn't be choosy. After all, he was doing what the Callers asked and they wanted this woman dead. Shrugging his shoulders, he waited for her to get in. He drove his trailer to another street not that far away and parked. He didn't want any witnesses spotting his vehicle if things didn't go smoothly. But he doubted they wouldn't. The Callers had always cleared his way, even going as far as disabling the alarm systems via utility poles' cables by blocking the alarm systems' communication with the company's service center.

All he had to do was enter the premises undetected and kill his targets. Easy as pie and just as sweet.

While he walked the block over to the house, his

thoughts roamed. The Callers had started talking to him almost five years ago on one of his darkest days. It wasn't that something catastrophic had happened to him that day. It was really an accumulation of all the shitty things that had occurred in his whole life. The shit piled so high, he wondered if he should keep on living or just end it all. He knew things would only get worse with time, not better.

But the Callers gave him a purpose in life, returned his will to live. Why they chose him to be their conduit, he didn't know. But thank God they did, because they saved him. And now as he walked over to the back of the house, he sighed deep, ready to act out their bidding.

His sinner was in the kitchen putting some groceries away. He observed her through the window with curiosity. She was cute and petite. Her chic suit probably designer made told him she was a businesswoman with expensive tastes. Nothing new there. But why did the Callers want her dead? He doubted it had to do with her taste in clothing.

When the phone rang, she picked up the cordless receiver, pinching it between her ear and shoulder while she took her food items out of her canvas carry bag. The window on the other side of the room must be open because Frank heard her voice loud and clear.

"Barry, why are you calling me here? What if John picked up the phone? You have to use my cell number."

Ah, adultery is the reason, he thought to himself.

But something didn't jive. His previous victims had committed more serious sins than that. It wasn't that he didn't see adultery as a sin. It was in his books, no doubt about it. But considering his past victims had been drug lords, crooks, and even murderers, an adulteress paled in comparison.

Just the same, it wasn't his place to judge his targets, just deliver their souls to the Callers for further judgment.

Taking a deep breath, he waited for the perfect time to make his move.

"Yeah, Barry. He'll be on the boat this weekend with his mistress. You ice him and make it look like she did it and I inherit everything. Then we head to Brazil."

He nodded as the picture became crystal clear. No, her sin was just up to par. Too bad her hunky muscle man puppet—he assumed he was that otherwise why would she even waste her time with him if he weren't—wouldn't be around for the same judgment she had coming her way.

It would have been nice to do a two-in-one killing tonight. Four months' withdrawal had him yearning for a double shot of his elixir. *Oh, well.*

When she hung up the phone and headed out the kitchen, he saw his window of opportunity. Putting on his gloves, he took one last look around to make sure no one had spotted him. The closest house stood twenty feet away. The lights were dark, the coast clear.

He slid out his Buck knife from his back pocket and folded open the sharp blade locking it in position. He jimmied the lock. The door soon clicked and opened when he turned the knob. When he didn't hear an alarm going off, he knew the Callers had cleared his way. *Good.*

Closing the door behind him, he quietly placed the knife on the counter and took out his strong cord from his shirt pocket. He tiptoed across the marbled floor heading to the corridor and saw her back while he advanced. She stood in the living room, holding the remote. She flicked the channels at record speed. She obviously wasn't skimming but searching for a specific station.

The lushly carpeted floor insulated his footsteps. A cat couldn't have moved quieter. He advanced with grace and precision. Each passing second felt like minutes with his snail's paced gait. The ticking clock marked his every step. He surmised it was a grandfather clock, probably in the living room. The air became cooler as he drew closer to climax. Was that Death's breath approaching he sensed?

When he finally got to just a few feet away from her, her potent perfume seeped into his nostrils urging him to sneeze. Wiggling his nose to stop it, he cursed to himself. Apparently some women didn't understand the term 'just a dab'. She must have poured half a bottle on herself this morning.

When she was dead and her body rotting, that perfume would probably kill the mortician unlucky enough to prep her for her funeral.

No matter how humorous the image of the mortician gagging and his eyeballs bulging out of his sockets was. He had a job to do. Pulling the cord taut, he quickly wrapped it around her neck and twisted her face toward him to see her fear as Death came to take her away.

Shockingly, he didn't see terror, but anger in her eyes. If he loosened the cord around her neck, he would have sworn she'd curse him for distracting her from her channel flicking task. But that annoyed look quickly swept away and utter panic came into play when she tried to take a breath and realized she had a cord blocking her windpipe. Her struggle lasted a few seconds only.

Yes, the excitement started then for Frank. That elixir of bliss slowly but steadily seeped out of her dying pores and into his, travelling into his veins and arteries. When it reached his heart, it fused with his blood making him stronger. Ecstasy of this kind could never be surpassed or bought on the streets. It needed to be taken by force.

Putting more pressure on the cord, he heard her gurgle for breath as her capillaries became visible in the whites of her pretty hazel eyes. Soon the veins in her neck expanded and she turned blue while the capillaries in her eyes got deeper red until they exploded making blotchy patches of red stains on her whites. The fireworks of life and death, this was it and it was beautiful.

It didn't take long for her life force to seep out of her and into Frank. Once she stopped breathing and her vacant bloody red eyes stared at nothingness, it ended. The elixir's flow ended, but he remained on a powerful high. If super villains existed, this was how they felt, no doubt in his mind.

He dropped her to the ground and quickly started his search. He had to leave the scene of the murder fast, but first he needed two very important things that he couldn't live without. As he rummaged around the living room, he sensed eyes boring through his back. He turned to gaze on her haunting face. All his dead victims looked at him with that expression that said they'd be waiting for him on the other side.

Good. He relished it. Might as well have a welcome party when he entered the gates of Hell. He never had one on Earth.

He walked over to her and nudged her face with the tip of his shoes so she faced the wall rather than him. As he did that something in his peripheral vision caught his eye, her purse on the corner table in the hallway. *Bingo!*

He walked over and picked it up. He swore the damn thing weighed twenty pounds. What the hell did she carry around with her? Opening it, a big makeup case obstructed his vision inside and he knew why it weighed so much. Underneath the gargantuan, impractical case, he saw it. A glimmering red burgundy baby calling his name.

Releasing a sigh, he slipped his fingers around it and pulled it out. A Nokia E63 GSM. He passed his index finger over the smooth casing and nifty keypad. The perfect piece to complete his collection. Bringing it up to his nose to smell it, he hoped it was new enough that the manufacturer's factory smell still lingered on it.

Unfortunately, all he got was a pungent whiff of her over-powering perfume. He rolled his eyes in disgust. This killing seemed bittersweet. He hoped the repulsive stench would dissipate with time. At least, it would be stored in a closed display case, so he wouldn't have to smell her every second of the day.

Now, for the final pièce de résistance. He walked back to the kitchen to get his knife and came back to her body. Was she right handed or left? He needed to know for sure before he started stabbing. Checking her middle fingers, he noted a tiny callous on her left one.

"There we go," he said smiling and then bit his lip when he made the puncture wound on her left index finger, the finger she used to type on her cell phone. The dead blood flowed slowly. He squeezed it and pressed it against the keys on the cell phone. When it dried, it would leave her bloody fingerprint on the trophy.

He waved it in the air and blew on it and within five minutes, it was dry enough for him to slip into a plastic protective bag and into his shirt pocket.

His mission complete, he headed out. He pushed the kitchen door curtain to the side to make sure no one was outside to spot his exit. When he saw nothing, he opened the door and slipped out. Walking in a casual gait, he headed back to his trailer. Even though he wanted to run the hell out of there, he couldn't risk drawing attention to himself.

The cool air caressing his heated cheeks and the full moon beaming on him, added the perfect ambiance to this evening.

When he came to the corner of the next street where he parked his trailer, he saw the empty all night diner and decided to go in when his stomach growled. A quick bite to eat and then he was out of this neighborhood.

The only waitress on duty glanced at him when he stepped in and motioned for him to take a seat anywhere. Being as the joint was empty, he took a seat up front where he had a clear view of the gorgeous full moon.

"What's your order, mister?" The gum chewing waitress asked while bringing him a glass of water.

He hadn't even had a chance to read the laminated menu on the table. How rude of her. A quick glance at the place told him the cook probably wasn't great, so the simplest of meals was his safest bet.

"A burger and a fry with a Budweiser." 'Please' was on the tip of his tongue, but considering her curt welcome, he decided to save it for a future day when the waitress actually deserved it.

She nodded and headed to the kitchen.

Alone at last. He took a deep breath, leaned on the cushioned back of the booth, and just savored the moment. Unfortunately, the moment was stolen from him as two policemen walked in.

A lump of air lodged in his throat as he followed their progress into the diner.

They both looked at him, nodding with slight grins. He reciprocated their gesture and picked up the menu. Better to look busy than have them stare into his eyes any longer.

Why the hell were they here? He doubted they were there on business, their gaits too casual for that. They took seats at the table closest to the door and began to chat amongst themselves.

When the waitress came out five minutes later carrying his order, she smiled and walked over to them, planting a kiss on one of the cop's lips. "Hey, honey."

"Hey, back, sweet thing," the dark-haired cop responded with the widest smile.

That answered his question. That lump in his throat loosened and slid down making breathing much easier.

"I'll be right back," she said as she walked over to Frank and placed his order on the table. "There you go, mister," she now said with a smile.

Hmm, amazing how people's behavior changes when given the right stimuli, Frank thought as he said, "Thanks."

Of course, when he saw the bloody burger and burnt

fries before him, he wanted to take back the word. But gazing at the cops chatting with the waitress told him they'd be there for a long time. And the cops looked like chatty folks, not the quiet loners he usually encountered at night.

He definitely didn't want the cops asking him questions. Hell no.

Taking the bloody burger in his hands, he brought it up to his mouth. Then the ringing started. He dropped the burger onto the plate in shock when the vibrating came after it.

With wide eyes, he stared at the cops. Thank God they didn't seem to hear it. Slipping his hand into his shirt pocket, he extracted the phone and slid it under the table, glancing at the lit screen. He could have sworn he had shut it off before placing it in the bag.

The number on the screen read unknown. When it rang a second time, he didn't waste any time tearing the bag open to retrieve the blasted thing to turn it off.

He sighed. *I knew I turned it off.*

Then it dawned on him. Knowing who was on the other end of the line and that they probably still had one more job for him, he placed the blood-stained, pungent perfume scented phone to his ear and answered the call....

Almost half an hour passed since Frank placed his call and yet no one had showed up. So much for planning his grand finale. And he thought this one last job would have been his best. Too late for regrets as there was no turning back now. Sighing as he stared at the full moon in the sky, he waited for what came next while coldness seeped into his bones.

From his peripheral vision, he noticed blue and red lights flashing. He turned his head slightly to peer at the night's horizon and realized company approached. He smiled faintly, knowing that just maybe the night wasn't ruined and the biggest high in history would soon be in his grasp.

Fatigue had begun to spread through him fifteen minutes ago and continued to weaken him, but that didn't stop him from relishing the drama about to unfold.

Forcing air into his lungs, he perked his ears to listen more closely and not miss any second of the juicy news coming to him.

After the police cruiser came to a halt a few yards away and two uniformed officers stepped out, surprise stunned him, and them.

Now isn't this the cherry on the cake, he thought to himself.

Speechless, he observed them through droopy lids.

"Holy Jeez!" one of the policemen cursed as he stared at him.

"What the hell?" the other man added.

Combing his fingers through his hair and staring at his partner, one of them said, "Pete, wasn't that the guy we saw at the diner?"

'Wasn't'? They apparently thought him already dead. Not wanting to burst their bubble, or his, he remained silent and still.

"Yeah, that was him, Jake." Pete nodded not breaking his focus from Frank's perch.

Pete quickly headed back to the patrol car. He obviously was calling in to report what was happening at the scene.

Drained of all energy, Frank's eyes slipped closed as his heart began to slow its beat. He heard footsteps approach the tower a few minutes later. Then the cop named Pete said, "They'll be here in a little bit."

"I guess we don't touch anything until the forensics unit has a chance to check things out," Jake said, walking closer to the tower. "Boy, look at the blood. Hell, he looks like a blinking Christmas tree with all those lit cell phones on him. How many do you think there is?"

Frank heard the cop named Pete come up next to Jake and respond, "I say over forty."

Actually, it was forty-five, but beggars couldn't be choosers. Pete was close enough.

"Shit, what was he trying to do?"

"Who the hell knows," Pete began to respond, then paused and added, "Hey, what's that clipped on his shirt?" He walked closer to Frank.

"Don't touch the crime scene, Pete," Jake shouted his warning. "Use a pen!"

Groaning, Pete responded, "I know. I'm not an idiot."

Frank felt a slight tug at his shirt, then it fell back into place a few seconds later.

"Well?" he heard Jake ask.

"I don't get it," Pete said.

"You don't get what? What did it say?"

"It said that his job was done and he needed to meet 'the welcome party' in Hell."

Jake snorted a laugh. "You never know what's going through these crazies' minds."

As much as Frank wanted to hear what Pete had to say next, time had run out. The show had finally ended and there would be no more applause or encores.

Exhaling his last breath, Frank bowed his head as the curtain closed for good.

<The Killers' Challenge>
Keith Gouveia

"Unbelievable!"

"What?" Peter asked, turning to his right to see Mike's computer screen.

For the past couple of nights the two sat, side-by-side, in front of the collection of monitors reading posts, instant messaging, and enjoying their creation. Despite his initial reservations, Peter had to admit his partner, for once, had a good idea.

"Mrdrman1968 is going around on the board questioning our abilities," Mike answered.

Peter leaned in and read the accusatory post. "Who does he think he is?"

"Or she."

Peter cocked his head and breathed through his nose, making a whooshing sound.

"Sorry," Mike said, and sheepishly turned away.

"We could kill on our own," Peter said, shaking his head at the idea that *he* needed Mike.

"We could?" Mike asked.

"Of course."

"I think you could, but me, I'm not so sure."

"You'd be fine," he said, but only half believing it himself.

"Oh great, now SexyMinx is taking his side."

"Or hers," Peter teased and Mike smiled.

"What are we going to do?"

"Who cares," Peter said, dragging the word. "We're never going to meet these people. Let 'em say what they want."

"Anything negative about us reflects on the site. We don't want that, do we? Not after all the work you put into it."

Peter sat there for a moment, staring at the red letters on a black background. *How dare they question my ability to hunt and kill. I don't need him. He needs me. Be lost without me. Don't these idiots know I can find each and every one of them and make them a permanent part of my collection?*

"What are you thinkin'?" Mike asked, breaking the silence.

"That we should answer this call."

"Seriously?"

"Yeah. The gauntlet's been laid down. If we are to remain masters of this domain, then we need to accept the challenge."

Peter's fingers began hammering away at the black keyboard in front of him. Two more messages appeared in response to Mrdrman1968's original post as he and Mike discussed their course of action. Lone stalkers from across the world contemplated on whether or not Peter and Mike could hunt, capture, and kill on their own. And which was the better of the two.

First, he thanked Mrdrman1968 for having the courage to call him out. Second, he wrote his eagerness to show beyond a shadow of a doubt that he and Mike, could in fact, kill solo. And lastly, he decided to make a game of it, and every game had a winner and a loser.

"What do you mean the winner collects his trophy of choice?" Mike asked after reading the rules Peter wrote.

"Simple, if I win, I pull one of your teeth. If you win, you can cut off one of my fingers."

Mike's eyes went wide. "Are you sure you want to do that?"

"What do I have to worry about?" he said with no regard to Mike's feelings.

Mike stared at his best friend with unblinking eyes. "You agree with them, don't you?"

Peter rolled his eyes and tilted his head away. "Don't be silly."

"You can't even look me in the eye when you say that. You think I need you. Probably think I'd get caught without you. Remember, it was my hand that killed Max!"

"Yeah," Peter said, turning back to face Mike, "and it was my quick thinking that kept your sorry ass out of juvie!"

"Oh, this is *sooo* on." Mike stood up and turned away from the computers. "You better start practicing how to hold a paint brush with one less finger."

"Where are you going?" Peter asked, partly guilty, partly curious.

"To get started."

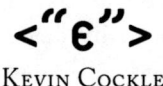

Kevin Cockle

Eric got out of the Caravan, glanced up and down the street. *Christ, I hate this neighborhood,* he thought. Old apartment buildings from the 1920s; once-stately houses from the same period that had been divided into separate apartments; an empty lot across the street, surrounded by the original low sand-stone and wrought-iron fencing of its glory days. To the north, the Calgary tower and clustered skyscrapers shone against dim stars—a dramatic contrast with the derelict residences that dated back nearly a century into the city's past. Two blocks down the street, Eric saw one of the district's male prostitutes wandering through the illumination of a street lamp, waiting to be cruised. Eric had parked under a burned out lamp, and knew he couldn't be seen from a distance. Pulling his collar up against a chill night breeze, he hurried through a broken gate, and up the steps towards the entrance of a dilapidated sandstone apartment building.

There was no security: Eric pulled the glass door open, bypassed the elevator he knew didn't work, and headed up the stairs. As he rounded the landing and approached the second floor, he could hear muted saxophone music from one of the rooms. He recognized the tune: *Harlem Nocturne*—one of his sister's favourites. He swallowed hard, made the second floor and headed down the hallway.

The music got louder as he approached. The other rooms on this floor were unoccupied—maybe even condemned—

but some landlord somewhere had found a way to make a profit on the place. The plumbing still worked; lights were good, but you might not want to plug anything into the ancient electrical sockets at this point.

Eric knocked quietly at 201; the music stopped. He reached into his pocket for his key, and let himself in.

The door opened directly onto a large, hardwood-floored living room illuminated by a single bare bulb in the overhead fixture. Erin, his sister, sat on a mattress covered in fleece sheets—her saxophone in her lap, her back to the off-white wall. A few boxes of her belongings lay open and pushed to the walls around the room; through a quaint archway Eric could see the dingy gas oven of the kitchen. His heart sank as it always did when he came here. *Jesus, Erin,* he thought.

"Hey babe," she said, her voice throaty from playing. She wore a midnight-blue satin camisole and panties that looked new and expensive, especially in contrast with the surroundings. Her coal black hair tumbled down her back in the usual haphazard tangles that somehow came across as deliberate. She set the sax down on the floor and grinned mischievously at him. "C'mere," she purred.

Eric glanced to his right, saw the bathroom door slightly ajar, the room dark behind it. His pulse quickened, and his sister said: "Deal with it later. Come here." She raised her arms above her head, waiting for him. "Leave the light on."

Eric fumbled with his shoes, hopping on one foot, then the other as he removed them standing up. He approached the mattress and knelt gingerly upon it, reaching to lift Erin's satin top up over her head and arms. Her pale body shone in the hard overhead light—muscular and lean where he was soft and heavy-set. She let her arms fall lightly around his neck, pulling him close. His hands cupped at her ribcage as they kissed, and the touch of her sinewy frame sent an electric thrill through his body.

All thought of the squalor, of the depths to which his sister had sank, evaporated as Erin twisted Eric to the mattress, and worked at the buttons of his shirt. His heart slapped in his chest, and his erection rose so suddenly against his jeans that it hurt.

And then he was lost—lost in the depths of her—drowning and rescued all at the same time.

As kids in elementary school, Erin had been protective of Eric, standing up for him in the schoolyard, her sheer ferocity often trumping the physical supremacy of various bullies. She was the extravert, the gymnast, the jock—older than he, more popular, smarter, though with little in the way of grades to show for it. She had always had a restless, wanton streak: stealing their parents' car when she was twelve years old— totaling it; caught with booze on school property in high school, earning a suspension for it. As they grew older, and her adventures grew more dangerous, he began to look out for her. "You're too wild for your own damn good," he'd often say.

"I'm wild, so you don't have to be," was her standard retort.

They made love on that sordid mattress, beneath that squalid light—he grunting softly with his exertions—she whining loudly, urging and clawing. He had never been with another woman—could not even imagine it. How could a stranger ever connect so perfectly with him? How could anyone else ever know him so completely?

It simply wasn't possible.

When they were finished, she lay drowsily on her belly to his left, her head towards his feet. Eric sat naked with his back against the coolness of the wall, his left hand massaging her right buttock. Sex-scent hung in the air: the room was warm, despite a cold February wind picking up outside, rattling the windows.

His eyes were drawn to the ornate tattoo that rose from

a point at her lumbar to her shoulder blades, gradually widening en-route to cover most of her back in a rough diamond shape. The motif was Haida Indian—the odd morphing-animal figures done in the style of West-Coast totem poles and paintings. It reminded Eric of his parents' living room with its Robert Davidson sculptures and prints. Purple shaded to mauve; cerulean blue shifted to indigo; pinks and reds and blacks filled out the palette. Her back shone with sweat under the white overhead light, giving the ink-work a high-gloss, hyper-real look. He wondered at the odd combinations of animals: sharks with sloped, human faces; rats with cat tails; ravens with batwings. Slicked up and shining, the figures seemed to writhe with alien life.

"What're you thinking?" she murmured, her head on her arms. He took in her long dark lashes, thought they made her look young.

"I'm thinking I've got to go to work in a few hours."

"Nuh-uh," she said. "You've got real work to do. You're phoning in sick."

"Fuck, Erin."

"Whatever. He's in the bathtub. I need you to get rid of the body."

Eric's eyes drifted to the open bathroom door; the long bar of darkness along its edge. When their parents had died, Eric had moved into the acreage out in Bearspaw. The house was a mansion by Calgary standards, on the outskirts of the city, isolated and situated on a good sized plot of land. He'd been disposing of Erin's handiwork for years out there: body parts in green garbage bags, buried, but not forgotten.

In the bathroom, he knew there would be saws, heavy rubber work-gloves, trash bags, and so on. Everything he needed to do the work.

She killed, and he looked after her.

When she killed, she needed him.

"Erin, I've got money," he whispered. "You don't need johns..."

"It's not a john," she said, irritated.

"Oh," Eric frowned, then thought of the prosti-boys outside, runaways, whatever. He had leapt to the conclusion that she had taken one of her customers, but of course, that wasn't necessarily the case. Once, because she was freelance, a pimp had moved on her, expecting to enforce his rights. The man had ended up in pieces, several feet below Eric's lawn. So no: it didn't have to be johns at all.

"Still, E. This place. I don't know why you don't come home and just let me..."

She laughed—a girly, giggling sound—and rolled onto her back, her hands behind her head in a way that flexed her compact, full little biceps. She placed a foot upon his chest and rubbed it there.

"Listen to you."

"What?"

"Like you don't love that I'm living here. Like you don't love that I hunt."

"I don't love it, Erin. I never have."

"E...come on," she smiled, and her brown eyes danced with malevolent humour. "You love it. You work in that fucking office of yours, filling out loan applications and credit card junk and RRSPs, and you love that deep down, you're different than all the other robots you work with, because you get to come here in the middle of the night and fuck your sister. Everything you do is safe, and predictable, except for me. If you didn't have me, what would you do?"

"Don't."

"What would you do?"

"Don't start."

"What. Would. You. Do?"

"I can't live without you."

Erin smiled. "Yeah," she said, her voice all bubble-gum and soda-pop.

He gazed at her gunslinger's eyes; her straight, pointed nose; those thin, sexy lips. "It's dangerous Erin," he said at last. "These are guys you're hunting. You're going to get hurt."

"You think so?"

"Well, what about last year? That guy who got the knife? You thought he was drugged, but he wasn't."

"Yeah," Erin grinned. "Close one!"

"Jesus."

Erin sat up cross-legged, leaning forward elbows-on-knees. Long tangles of damp black hair tumbled across both breasts. "I'm not really in as much danger as you think, E." Her voice low, conspiratorial.

"So you think."

"No...really. Haven't you ever wondered how I do it? How I've done it all this time? And never so much as a scratch on me?"

"Roofies." Eric shrugged, bewildered.

"That's after. But before, when I hunt, I'm all animal baby."

Eric thought immediately of her Haida tattoo art. Erin smiled.

"I'm wild, but with you, I'm tame. You gettin' it?" She prodded, eyes fixed upon his.

"I know you think you're..."

"I'm a shape shifter, E. Ever since mom and dad died, I've been able to go all the way...swap my skin. I spot them from the air as a crow; stalk them as a jaguar; take them down pure nature-channel, baby. Trust me: these boys never have a chance."

Eric was rarely afraid of his sister, but he was often afraid *for* her. Staring into her eyes, and seeing her absolute belief in her own fantasy, he realized for the first time that

Erin was truly, deeply, disturbed. Not for killing in the first place—he had long ago rationalized that away, given her circumstances. Killing almost had a logical justification, living on the edge as she did. But this, this idea that she changed shapes, took the form of animals to better hunt her prey...that was psycho-ward stuff.

"Erin," he said. "Come home with me."

She smiled up at him through her eyelashes, her chin tilted down. She reached up with her left hand to caress his jaw line ear-to-chin. After a while she whispered: "You want to be a zoo-keeper."

"No, that's..."

"Shhh," she said, trailing a fingertip across his lips. "You think control would make you happy, but I promise you E, that's not the answer."

"I just want you to be safe."

She smirked. "Safe is code for caged." She leaned in to kiss him then, ending the argument. Pulling back, she said in her softest voice: "Get rid of the body, E. Two hours 'til dawn. I'll call you."

Erin had a range of voices—strident; purring; whining; brazen; silken; hurt; hurtful. But her soft voice, the peculiar tone of soft she used, was the voice that always got its way.

Like the time she said of their parents: "They're on to us, E. They know. If I don't do something soon, they'll split us up. You know they will." Oh yes, that voice had been very soft indeed.

Eric rose from the mattress and proceeded to do as he had been told.

Days passed.

Burying the bodies was the easiest part. The property to the west of the city was surrounded by trees—only a spy satellite could have seen him. Six reinforced garbage bags sectioned the body out head, arm, arm, leg, leg, trunk: same way, every time. He emailed the branch at 4:30AM so his manager could see the time, and explained that he was ill. It would be fine: his uncomplaining hours of unpaid overtime always kept him in the good-books. Then, when he was finished by 10:00, he got himself together and went in around noon anyway—just to be heroic. The effort was noticed, and appreciated. His lack of sleep was interpreted as legitimate, non-specific illness.

On the weekends, he headed to the library to bone up on Haida art and mythology. Cosmological reasoning left him dazed: he really couldn't get his head around it. In an enchanted, non-Newtonian universe, so it seemed, all things were alive; all things possessed a kind of sentience, and were interconnected. All men were possessed of an animal spirit and were imbued with animal traits, but some men could slip their skins and become animal outright. Reality wasn't as locked down for the Haida as it was for the Europeans; there was free play of "signifiers" over "signifieds"—a constant shifting of meaningfulness. Whatever that meant. Eric was frankly baffled that any people could believe such ideas, and frankly horrified that his own sister apparently did. In any event, he couldn't make heads or tails out of it.

A more useful resource was the Snuff Syndicate website. On the surface, the website, like many other serial-killer themed sites, contained plenty of historical data, forensic techniques, and psychological analysis for the interested viewer. Unable to take his sister to see a real professional, Eric found the peculiar authoritativeness of the site compelling, and tried to learn all he could about the nature of psychotic breaks.

If he'd had the courage, he would have gone onto the message board—but there was no telling how secure it really was, or how monitored. Rumours swirled that actual predators frequented the board—protected by all manner of encryption; floating servers; international domain codes and so on. To be able to talk with one would have been invaluable, but there was no way. Erin was the risk-taker in the family: Eric would freeze up just thinking about going through the log-in procedure.

He got back to his routine easily enough. He worked at a branch of a large bank, located in a small strip mall, and had settled long ago for permanent mid-tier management status. Higher than a teller, he was lower than branch manager, and was happy to soldier on in that capacity. He had a small office; arranged loans and investments for customers; worked longer hours than were required—even weekends during RRSP season—and was considered a model employee. Quiet and courteous, he was well-liked if essentially unknown: the consummate professional.

Which is why, when he arrived at work on February 14th, he was stunned to see a small glass paperweight with a rose frozen inside, holding down a Valentine's Day card atop his desk. He stood and blinked from the doorway, then stepped to the desk, picked up both objects, and stared at them as though they were alien artifacts.

"Happy Valentine's Day, Eric!" A woman's voice said from behind him. He turned and saw Esther Sawyer in a tan blouse and skirt, smiling expectantly at him. She was a relatively new hire—still in her probationary period, and because of his long service, Eric did most of the basic training for the branch. She'd been under his wing for a little over a month now.

She'd been flirty with him from the onset. She was pretty in a big-boned, friendly sort of way—not at all the sort of thing he was used to. She wore her mousy brown hair in a ponytail and was always smiling. Customers loved her, though her attention to detail wasn't all that great. Still— she had potential.

He'd enjoyed the banter, but shied away when she'd

asked him out to drinks with some of the other tellers after work. "Eric never comes for drinks," Leslie—another bank-lifer—had chimed. Eric had smiled, and shrugged his way out of it. But Esther had persisted, so much so that there was *talk*, apparently, in the office. Eric was equal parts appalled, embarrassed, and thrilled by the attention.

"Look," Esther said, stepping into the office, her hands clasped together at her chest. "I know this is a little forward, but jeez, guy, you just don't take a hint! I mean...what does a girl have to do?"

Eric chuckled, fumbling for words. Esther cut him off.

"One dinner. It's Valentine's Day, Eric, you don't want me to be alone on Valentine's Day, do you? If you're freaked out, I'll understand, but I really, *really* hope you're game. Hey? What do you say?"

Eric swallowed. His sister was always telling him to go out: "You're a good looking guy," she'd say after screwing his brains out, relaxing and chatting. "We'll always have each other, but a little something on the side would be good for you, bro'."

That's what she *said,* but Eric wasn't convinced. Maybe she said such things because she knew he'd never go through with it. He'd never been aroused by the sight of another woman; never had the impulse to be involved with anyone else. Deep down, he wondered if his sister truly wanted him to experience other women. There was a specialness to it being just the two of them, forever. Then again, his sister was anything but a Valentine's Day style romantic. Maybe she really did want him to get out a little. Lord knows *she* did.

Esther was waiting—her lips set in a little half smile; eyebrows raised.

"Sure," Eric said. "No, I'd love to."

"Awesome!" Esther peeped. "Pick me up at seven. I've made reso's for seven-thirty."

"Oh my God, I love this place!" Esther had said when they arrived. The restaurant was dark, romantic—all cherry-wood hues and dark violets, arranged in chimney-atrium style on three art-deco floors. Eric had read about the place in the paper, knew it was one of Calgary's best new restaurants.

He'd thought about calling Erin for some advice on cologne and dress, but then decided to call her afterward, once it was all over. It would be fun to go over the date with her; she'd be proud of him, probably a little amused. Maybe just a touch jealous, Eric hoped, though she probably wouldn't show it right away. She'd probably make some joke about Esther's hips or something, just to let him know she cared.

He'd picked Esther up exactly at the specified time—in the Corolla of course, not the Caravan. The Caravan was for *work*. He'd pulled her chair out for her; ordered the wine for both of them, taking command as he knew a man should, as Erin would. Esther was delighted, charmed: she laughed easily, and too loudly for the setting, apparently without caring in the slightest. In charming her, Eric found himself being charmed: she grew more attractive, the more she seemed to respond to him.

They chatted about work, gossiping about co-workers, bitching about the bank's oppressive compliance and restrictive working atmosphere. In actual fact, Eric didn't mind the highly structured bank culture—appreciated the widely documented and clearly understood rules. But he hammed it up for Esther—rolling his eyes when appropriate—even risking the odd swear word at times, just to show how edgy he could be outside of the office.

Before he knew it, they'd finished off a bottle of Pinot; gotten to nine o'clock without so much as a break in the conversation, and were sharing a rich frozen nougat desert over a couple of glasses of good port. As far as Eric could tell, he was having a great time.

"So," Esther said with a playful grin as she took in a spoonful of dessert, "how come you're not married, hey? Good looking guy; good job; what're you, some kind of player?"

Eric smiled. "Dodged a couple bullets, I guess," he said. "There was somebody once...but, you know. Just didn't work out."

"Tell me about it!" Esther laughed, tapping atop the knuckles of his left hand with her fingertips. She'd been tapping and touching at him all night long. "Any family in town?"

Eric double-clutched instinctively, then relaxed. "One... sister," he said, adding: "We're not close."

"That explains it then."

"Explains what?"

"Why nobody would know you even had a sister. Jeez... you're so secretive! I couldn't find out anything about you from anybody."

He shrugged. "Just busy, you know, at work. Not much for small talk, I guess." He felt his phone vibrate in his jacket pocket. Eric frowned and thought about ignoring it.

"I've got a brother and two sisters," Esther said. "My brother's like this big lawyer in Edmonton, and he's older than us right? So it's like he's our boss or dad or something, so I'm like..."

The phone continued to vibrate. Eric interrupted Esther's spiel: "I've...I'm sorry E, I've got to take this call."

"E? Oh my God...we've already got pet names for each other? Hey, you're, E, too!"

Eric blushed, suddenly flummoxed by his faux-pas. *Talk about a Freudian slip!* He rose from the table, fumbling for the phone, heading to the bathroom with a frown. Once he was safely out of view, he reviewed a text from Erin: "I'll need you tonight. Usual time, E."

Damn.

Of all the nights for Erin to hunt, she had to pick *this* one. Three-hundred and sixty-four other nights in the year, and there would have been no conflict. Eric closed the phone and stood staring at himself in the mirror for a moment. He saw Erin's aquiline nose, and her thin lips, but the curly brown hair belonged to his father as did the clumsy, bear-like frame. Erin was all lithe, ballistic power: he was roley-poley in comparison, although tall enough to carry the weight well. She'd gotten their mother's music; he'd gotten their father's math. Gathering himself, he left the bathroom with a stern expression.

Returning to Esther, Eric said: "I...bad news. My sister's been in an accident."

"Oh my God!" Esther blurted, eyes wide.

"It's not serious, but...I...I've got to go get her. I'm the only family in town."

"Oh my God, of course."

"I'm really sorry Esther."

"Don't be silly...I had a great time. Didn't you have a great time?"

"I did! Yes, I did. I'm sorry."

"Nope, it's fine. We'll get the bill and we'll go. But there's gonna be a round two mister...don't you worry!"

He dropped her off at home and was startled when Esther leaned across the seat and gave him a quick peck on the cheek. She winked at him and let herself out before he could rally and get out to open the door for her. He watched her heading up the walk to the 70s style duplex, and waved when she turned to wave at him. *That was fun,* he thought to himself, relieved it was over.

9:30 PM. He had to get back out to Bearspaw; drink some coffee to get rid of the wine-buzz he had going; change; get the Caravan; then drive back to Erin's. He'd get there around ten to two; fuck Erin until three or so; process the body, and get out of town before sunrise. *At least it's a weekend*, Eric thought. He didn't like to call in sick more than once a month.

"What the hell took you so long?" Erin snarled when Eric arrived. She wasn't ready for him, wasn't dressed for him: she still wore her black jeans, pink tank top, and the short black leather jacket he'd given her for her birthday ages ago. Her dark eyes blazed as she stalked the room, her cowboy boots sounding out loud against hardwood.

"What are you talking about?" Eric said: it was the usual time. He'd never been late for anything in his whole life. He glanced around the room: her few boxes of possessions where tied up and ready to move. The sheets were off the mattress, leaving it as bare as the single bulb in the ceiling.

"We've got to move, E," Erin said, her voice tight with urgency.

"Why? What happened? Are you okay?" Eric fought down sudden panic at the thought of his sister's overconfidence coming back to haunt her. One of these days, one of these guys was going to surprise her.

She stared at him, seething. "You really don't know. You stupid shit: you really have no fucking clue, do you?"

"What? Jesus, Erin, what's the problem?"

"Go into the bathroom. Check it out. Go."

Eric frowned. The door to the bathroom was closed.

"GO!" Erin shouted, then paced the floor, running her fingers through long black tangles.

Eric crossed to the door, opened it, slapped on the light.

In the bathtub, lay Esther Sawyer in a loose-limbed sprawl. Hair obscured her features; her head lolled forward at an unnatural angle, courtesy of her broken neck. She still wore her left pump, the right having been lost in transit, apparently.

"Jesus Christ," Eric breathed, staring. *Erin's never taken a woman before,* was his first thought. Then the confusion hit him. *How did she know...?*

Erin poked her head in the doorway, leaning on the frame outside. "Yeah: she's a cop, idiot."

"What the hell are you talking about?" Eric said, turning on the spot.

"She's a cop. You fucking moron. She's an undercover cop."

"You're out of your mind," Eric said, before he could take it back. "She's a teller."

"UNDERCOVER teller. We've got to get a move on. Slice and dice bro', then let's bolt."

The room was spinning around Eric; he felt sick to his stomach. He turned back to Esther, trying to remember her at work; remembering her at dinner. She'd been asking about him. Snooping. But she'd been interested in him... hadn't she? He could just picture her asking some of the other girls: "So what's his story?"

But she was a new hire, and not particularly adept at the window, despite having been at it for a few weeks. Could she really have been a cop? And if so, how had Erin found out?

There was a loud bang from the front room; a cracking and shattering of wood.

Footsteps thudded on the hardwood floor: many footsteps from many feet.

"DOWN! GET DOWN!" A husky voice shouted. "GET DOWN YOU SICK FUCK!"

"Shoot the cocksucker."

"That's enough sergeant: take him down. Do NOT kill him."

"One move. Just one move, cocksucker. Do something."

Eric turned slowly in the bathroom doorway, raising his hands slowly to shoulder height. Half a dozen SWAT team members had piled into the room, taking up firing positions with semi-automatic weapons. Behind them, men in trench coats with ear mikes fanned out, calling the shots. Eric assessed them as feds—maybe even American: it was not unusual for Canadian cities to call on the FBI in cases such as these.

Eric glanced around the room. "Where's my sister?"

"On the floor, fuck. Won't tell you again," commanded one of the officers.

"Sir, I thought Esther said—"

"That's right," said the man who was obviously in charge, gun still trained on Eric. "There are no records of him having a sister."

"Liars!"

"Floor...NOW."

Figuring he had said too much already, Eric lowered himself to his right knee, then onto his stomach as the men moved in. He put his hands behind his back, rested his left cheek against the floor in a kind of slow motion shock.

One man secured his wrists. Another cursed at the sight of a fellow officer lying dead in the bathtub. Eric lay very still, assuming that it was 50-50 whether or not he'd make it into custody alive.

Across the room, Eric saw movement against the far wall. Focusing, he could see a tiny grey body—a mouse—scampering along the molding toward the kitchen door. Without being seen, it made the doorway, and scuttled onto linoleum, rounding the corner to evade detection.

Eric smiled.

It was true. She had them all fooled.

His sister *was* a shape shifter. She'd made it into the kitchen as a mouse, gotten away clean. Right underneath the noses of Calgary SWAT and the FBI!

They had nothing on him: he hadn't even touched Esther's corpse; was just as surprised by it as they were.

They'd grill him, and then they'd let him go. They'd have to.

Go, baby. Hide. I'll shake these clowns, then come get you.

I'll take you home for a while.

Just for a little while.

I'll take you home and keep you safe.

<Alone in the Night>
Keith Gouveia

Mike slinked out from the underbrush. He had spent the last hour and a half hiding. His eyes on the one storey ranch before him. The house was dark, the last light extinguished nearly forty minutes ago.

Doesn't feel right, Mike thought as he stepped up to the back door.

Twice—while waiting for the Buffords to go to bed—he looked over his shoulder, expecting to see Peter right there beside him. Both times he found he was alone.

Stupid message board. Stupid members.

Mike analyzed the door handle, then reached into the inside pocket and selected the size seven tubular lock pick. He wasn't as skilled as Peter, but he was confident he could pick the lock without him.

How could my brothers and sisters do this to me? he wondered as he inserted the tool into the slot.

One-by-one, the lock pins were slowly pushed down as the rod was pushed deeper into the mechanism. When all the pins broke the shear plane, the lock disengaged and Mike stepped inside.

After just a few paces into the living room, Mike bumped into an end table and quickly stifled a forthcoming yelp. He stood still, gaze locked on the archway to the main hall, waiting for a sign of movement.

This is why we don't rush these things. First time alone, first mistake.

He stood there another moment, contemplating calling it quits and admitting that he could not do it alone, but he thought back to the first night he and Peter shared after Max's death. Peter had trusted him then, and continued to trust him with his life after all these years. Each saw a piece of themselves in the other.

That says something, doesn't it? he told himself. *If Peter didn't think me capable, he wouldn't give me the time of day. I have to do this. Or he'll lose respect for me.* The lyrics to Pink Floyd's "Wish You Were Here" played out inside his mind, calming his nerves.

His head nodded to the imaginary beat. *Two lost souls swimming in a fish bowl...*

With his confidence refocused, Mike ventured down the hall and toward the bedrooms.

In the pocket on the right side of his jacket, Mike's serrated knife lay in wait for its master's hand. He reached in and grabbed hold of it as he peered through the ajar bedroom door.

Perfect, he thought, seeing Mr. and Mrs. Bufford fast asleep. Across the hall, the Bufford's little boy slept soundly as well. *Sorry kiddo, Mom and Dad first.*

Mike wasn't as righteous as Peter—making the world a better place one asshole at a time—and his selection process was simple; with their ten acres of land, the unfortunate family posed little risk. He could take his time, enjoy the kill, and should he fumble as he suspected the others expected, he'd have plenty of time to escape, and the safety of the neighboring woods to flee to. He could hide in the dense forest for days living off the land, feeding on grubs and berries.

Nudging the door open further, Mike stepped into the room. Moonlight filtering in through the window refracted off the blade's surface as he walked up along the bedside. His plan was simple, stab Mr. Bufford in the heart, then move to Mrs. Bufford, and then finally their son. With the deed done, he'd then have all the time needed to set the stage.

When writing the rules of the game, Peter had tipped the odds in his favor. The scoring factors were three fold: level of difficulty; speed of execution; and artistic flair. There was no way Mike could compete with Peter's ability with a brush. The patience Peter exuded for those minute details were beyond him, but he remembered the newspaper article that set their lives on its current path.

Oliver Hewitt was an artist dabbling in paintings and sculptures. He arranged his victims with an artistic flair, one Mike thought he could recreate. But there was only one sculpture that would resonate with Peter—that would garner his respect.

Salivating at the thought of Peter conceding defeat, Mike plunged the blade of his knife all the way to the hilt into the heart of Mr. Bufford. The body twitched, the left hand smacking the limp arm of Mrs. Bufford as the final breath passed over his lips.

"What is it?" She rolled over, eyes fluttering as if she were trying to adjust to the darkness.

Mike pulled out the blade and Mrs. Bufford's scream turned to a raspy gasp as the knife pierced her bosom and penetrated her heart.

Her brow wrinkled, eyes squinted and lengthened the crow's feet in the corners, and her lips pursed until the pain washed away, and her facial features relaxed as death claimed her.

"Mommy?"

Mike turned around, pulling his knife free from the carcass to see a little boy standing in the doorway, rubbing his eye with one hand and clutching a fuzzy teddy-bear in the other. The plush toy's legs barely hovered above the floor.

Damn kid, Mike thought, stepping toward him. *It would have been better if you'd stayed asleep.*

<snuffingly yours>
J. T. Seate

As Tamara wheeled into an available parking spot, the front door at the Lancer Bar swung open. A couple, arm in arm, descended the steps, laughing. Tamara could hear the backbeat of a saxophone and laughter—two earthy fundamental sounds of an active city. She imagined what was to come this night and the primal need in her reared its head and yearned for fulfillment.

She'd been driving around thinking about all the men in the city who were sitting quietly or lying in their beds, breathing softly in the night with dreams of sleeping with a pretty girl. The image aroused her as she wondered who might tickle her fancy next and what approach she might take.

She watched as another couple entered the bar. The man moved his hand to the woman's breast and gave it a playful squeeze before they tossed their cigarette butts and went inside. Tamara squeezed her breast and felt a tingle run through her body as her nipple stiffened inside her blouse. She imagined it between the thumb and forefinger of an excited male who would be thinking about what her body would hold in store. Her need proved stronger than her ever-vigilant caution, and she climbed out of her car.

The Lancer Bar was located in a section of town called The Heights, a moniker much loftier than it deserved. The neighborhood fell in and out of favor, depending on what commercial endeavors happened to occupy the area at the time. The bar had weathered the ebb and flow of popularity and could currently be classified as a flourishing yuppie joint.

Inside the Lancer, Tamara perused the place and sized up its patrons with wise and observant eyes. There were a few macho assholes making their moves like birds looking for a place to perch, but most of the men were just half-drunk guys scratching their asses and hoping. The men and women were all determined to enjoy themselves with loud talk and drink, and maybe more if they played their cards right. She spotted a couple of air-headed bimbettes cruising for free drinks and chose to check out the scene from the opposite end of the bar.

Tamara sensed the attention of a few shift to her. She paused, feeling sniffed at like a dog in a strange neighborhood. A good-looking guy sat at the bar solo. He looked the part of a young corporate type with a frosty glass of beer and a bowl of pretzels in front of him. A ballgame was on above the bar, but he didn't appear interested. He clearly wasn't drunk. That was good. Tamara didn't like sloppy. Even though he wasn't yakking it up like everyone else, she guessed that he would jump at company. She planted her fanny on the stool next to him and ordered a Lime Coke.

She was wearing a low-cut black silk top without a bra, and a black skirt. He was unable to prevent his eyes from taking a visual survey down her body. Following the brief journey, he looked at the profile of her face. He wasted no time. "My name's Larry. Can I offer you something more interesting than a coke?"

She turned on the stool so he could get a good look at her legs as she crossed them, vamping him just a bit. Their eyes locked as she observed him with unblinking, green-eyed solemnity. "I have my vices, but alcohol isn't one of them."

"Then why come to a bar?"

"Same as you."

"And that is?"

"You don't want to face the quiet. Not yet anyway. You need people and a few laughs. A drink or two. Or maybe even just one person."

"Is that an offer, Miss…?"

"My name's Judy. I saw you at the bar and was overwhelmed with lust."

"You're teasing me."

"A little, but not much. I guess it *is* an offer."

"You're not a…?"

"A working girl?" Tamara smiled teasingly. "I'm not a hooker. I'm not into economics, but I am, however, into spontaneity."

Larry smiled at her candor. "Because of the murders, a lot fewer guys are picking up chicks these days."

"Terrible, isn't it? I guess us girls are going to have to work harder."

"Well, it *is* a little scary."

"Afraid I'm the Bludgeoning Bunny?"

"That's cute. Not as cute as the Sex-Kitten Killer though. The press seems to think she might be a prostitute with a chip on her shoulder."

"Some chip, putting a bullet between men's eyes. What sort of mind could do such a thing?"

"I guess there are sick puppies of both sexes. I mean, men have sex with women and then kill them all the time. Why should a switch-a-rooney be so surprising? Probably abused when she was young."

"Few people can control their desires, so it's a waste of time to second guess them." She sipped her Coke and leaned toward him revealing more freckled cleavage. "Hey, neither of us came here tonight to discuss sex and death. How about just sex?"

"It's my favorite subject." Larry glanced at Tamara's curvy body in the black ensemble. "You're an interesting girl, Judy."

"It's too bad you're wearing your scaredy-pants because I'm in the mood for love tonight." She looked at him and allowed the corners of her mouth to create a petulant smile. "And I like the way you look at me."

"No guts, no glory," he said. "Maybe if I could frisk you?"

Tamara laughed. "We'll see." She lifted her glass. "Here's to mistakes and lucky breaks, whichever the case may be."

He did the same. "Here's to moving on."

They finished their drinks. Tamara got basic directions to his place and told him she would follow in her car. When she slid off the stool, she let her breasts graze Larry's arm. She didn't want him to get distracted by something flashier. They split with him trailing a few steps as life moved on for everyone else in the bar. She climbed into her nondescript, late model sedan and stayed close behind his taillights.

The standard bar hook-up was risky—too many people, but she was careful about changing her appearance with hair and makeup.

Finding men was a game Tamara had begun playing long ago. In high school, her desire had started with steamy paperbacks in which bosoms heaved and bodices were lustily ripped open. By her senior year, she'd slept with the football captain, the class president, and gave some consideration to a hunky PE coach. But it might have made headlines and rained on everyone's parade.

By college, her curiosity had surrendered to new variations on the sexual theme and she was now a slave to those passions. She occasionally indulged in S&M, but even that had not completely quenched her curiosity. Although curiosity supposedly killed the cat, the cat and mouse game was thrilling. And, unbeknownst to her prey, it was she that was the cat. And somewhere, deep inside. She wanted to do more than have sex with them. Much more.

But there was another influence in Tamara's life. She'd met someone at a self-defense class and they had become close. Her presence and opinions mattered and Tamara wondered what Freda might think of her actions.

Tamara parked behind Larry in his driveway. The house was a spacious one story in the nicer part of the Heights.

"I take it you live alone?" she asked.

"I have a roommate, but he's out for the evening."

"That's convenient," she said.

"Very."

Larry offered Tamara a drink, but she declined. Instead she said. "If it's all the same to you, I'd just as soon dispense with the small talk, see what you've got to offer? Take me to your bedroom."

"This is my lucky night." He watched her nipples distend against her blouse with anticipation. "What I need more than anything is a beautiful woman for the night." He led her to the bedroom where Tamara slipped out of her garments.

"What do you think?" she asked and struck an artistic pose.

"God, you're gorgeous. Where have you been all my life?"

"No need to cliché me. It doesn't have to be love. It can just be fun."

"I guess you're not a Black Widow after all?" he answered as he undressed.

"How would you know? Like the Black Widow, the Sex-kitten Killer has sex first and kills later."

"So how does she get away with it?"

"Easy. Gets away with it by being smart and careful. By planning ahead."

"And dead men tell no tales," Larry said with a smile. "I better check you for weapons."

"I guess you better."

He gently rubbed a finger along her clitoris and smiled as her body trembled to the touch. "No hidden weapons. Only very tempting body parts."

"Then it's only you who has a weapon. Let's see how skilled you are with it."

Their lips slid together. His penis touched her belly. She didn't fight her needs, whatever they might be. With unchecked urgency, she fondled his manhood. He bit his lip and held his breath in rapture.

"Tag, you're it," she said to him.

He lifted her with unconscious roughness. She wrapped her legs around his waist and locked her ankles behind him. He was a fulcrum while she was the hinge.

Tamara sighed at the feeling of immediate consumption while Larry stumbled to the bed with her in tow and sat down. She raised her legs so he could lie on his back, still inside her. There were few words between them, but the breathing was heavy. The friction was in the right place.

"You're great," Larry gratuitously offered.

"Thanks," Tamara replied as the friction between their tufts of hair increased.

She trembled like a virgin about to taste love for the first time. She looked at the ceiling rather than at him as she imagined all those men at home in their beds without her and thought about how she would treat all of them the same as she did Larry if only she had the opportunity.

Larry bathed in the scent of her arousal. He gritted his teeth as he approached climax. Tamara worked her pelvis up and down, side to side. Her motion shifted into high gear. She leaned forward and put her forearm against his throat, not applying pressure, but thinking about it.

When she'd had enough, she leaned back on her hands and moved her hips as fast as she could to bring forth her own starburst. Her orgasm strained for release. And finally, the payoff came. Her legs clamped against his thighs to hold him deep as she jerked with each spasm. She felt like a triumphant goddess riding the winds as she came. She emoted with a shuddery sigh of satisfaction.

With a jerk and a shudder, he soon erupted inside her, groaning with pleasure.

After her orgasmic explosion, she decided he was an okay guy and remained on top of him as he trembled with small aftershocks. Then she collapsed on top of him, momentarily paralyzed.

"You may not be a killer," Larry said, "but you're a regular sex-kitten."

"Sweet as pie and tough as nails, that's me," she said in a post-coital drowse. She worshipped her independence, but she also loved the thrill of the brief interlude, her femininity affirmed. But following the release and initial internal warmth, another set of emotions sometimes took over. Sometimes the quenching of desire lead to an unladylike emotional pattern. The power and righteousness some of her lover's derived from their achievement could simmer to a boil and develop into a rage within her. She didn't psychoanalyze it or fight it. She didn't care why. It just was. A certain word or act could make the difference in whether they lived to talk about having sex with her or not. While her torso flattened out against Larry's chest and their breathing slowed, that decision was yet to be made.

No sooner had she reached the opinion that her night with Larry was about no more than hot sex, an ominous feeling overcame her, a keen sense of impending danger. She heard a sound near the bedroom door and turned her head to look. A man stood in the dim light, watching them. How long had he been there, she wondered. "Who's this? A cop?" The words were out of her mouth before she thought.

"Cop?" Larry said. "Hell no. Tony and I just watch each other's back nowadays."

"I dig," Tamara said. "But I'm not too keen on group sex."

"Don't worry. Tony was just a happy observer. He'll keep his distance if that's the way you want it."

"And you do the same for him?"

"We alternate going out. Then we call to let the other know we're coming home with a guest. And you know the rest."

Her momentary lapse of liking Larry was replaced by a hard, clean rage, one which went beyond a purple curtain in her mind and saw life and death in a new light.

Tony was a dark and wiry looking Italian-type. She'd been scared when he'd first appeared in the doorway, and his presence would call for a slight adjustment to her plan. He was fully dressed. She liked variety and might have been willing to fuck Tony also, but it would have given Larry the chance to get away and she couldn't let that happen.

"I hope it was as good for you as it was for us," Larry said to Tony and wiggled his eyebrows at Tamara like in an old Groucho Marx movie.

"You know it."

Whoever said mood swings were rational? The line between love and hate could be oh, so thin. If Tamara had had any doubts, the eyebrow gesture sealed the deal. "You were fantastic, Larry. Maybe I can be a bitch-kitty with Tony another time."

Tony slid around the room like an oil spill. He walked to the lump on the chair that was Tamara's purse. He picked it up. "Just a little look-see," he said.

"You'll be disappointed. No gun, no knives, no num-chucks."

Satisfied with the search, he stepped aside while Tamara got off the bed and headed toward her pile of clothes.

"It's been a real pleasure, Tamara," Larry said as he placed his arms behind his head, not caring to cover himself. He felt in control, demonstrating his superiority even now. "There's more where this came from, so drop by sometime." His lips twisted into a faint smirk. "One of us is usually home."

It was Tamara's turn to smile. She made her thumb and forefinger into a pistol and pointed it at the two men. "Tag, I'm it."

When Tamara was safely inside her apartment, she reflected on the satisfying moment following her final emotional release inside Larry's house. The lust-rage had been successfully unleashed for now and she felt calm. She stepped out of her dress and removed the small, shiny item from the pocket sewn just above the hemline of her skirt. She rubbed the bulb of the silencer mounted on the tiny pistol between her thumb and forefinger.

She had never killed a man she hadn't slept with until tonight, but Larry and Tony had left her little choice. While the two of them laughed and joked about another conquest, she had played along. Then she calmly removed her little protector from its hiding place in the hem of her dress and planted a quick, single shot into Tony's forehead and one more into the second silly, smirking face. She'd washed off Larry's naked body and wiped the place for fingerprints. She was dressed and gone before the first light of day.

Tamara drank a glass of cold milk then took a hot shower, washing away any possible remaining trace of Larry from her body. Then she gazed at herself in the bathroom mirror. Her body smooth, supple, and clean, ready for what would come next.

She scurried into her bedroom, taking the gun with her and climbed in bed, naked. She rubbed the barrel of the silver pistol against her thigh. On Monday, she'd go back to work as the demure business woman with the big, round glasses. But tonight she'd fall asleep thinking about how the city paper's next edition would describe the latest escapade of the Sex-Kitten Killer.

Freda's hand closed over the hand holding the pistol. "How did it go, sweetie?" she asked.

"I ran into the Dynamic Duo," Tamara answered. "I took both of them down."

Freda rose up on her elbow. "You're kidding?"

"The guy was scared of bringing home the Sex-kitten. His roomie was playing babysitter." She couldn't keep from smiling. "Even an insect that destroys the male after coupling can't claim a double-header."

"They're all guilty as sin. Did you have sex with both of them?"

"That would have been awkward. Left one wet and one dry. But both went out with smiles on their faces."

"I bet he wanted to. I could have made it a foursome. You should have called."

"We're going to have to be more careful than ever. The guys are suspicious of all us little flirts now."

"Stay careful and safe. Let's not blow it now by getting careless." Tamara laid the gun aside so her hands could be free to explore Freda.

"You change the plates?" Freda asked.

"Everything was handled like you posted on the Snuff Syndicate, you sexy minx."

"Just my cop's mind talking. I'll make sure my next one lives alone," Freda said. "Get more than one of them in a room and it's all about macho."

"There was a benefit in snuffing more than one. *Two* new nipples for our little collection," Tamara said with a grin.

"Guess calling us 'The Nipple Killer' would be too racy for the headlines. They're keeping that little tidbit under wraps at the station."

Tamara stretched and yawned. "Male cops think the same way as our perps, I'm sure. They think all a woman really needs is to have her pump primed. Once their little brains take over, men are easy to nail."

"Their eyes are hardwired to their crotches. I'm not sure their brains are ever involved."

Both women laughed. Tamara said to Freda. "There apparatus does have its rewards, but they're the ones who practice the bloody game."

"The bastards. But as amusing as they are, I always look forward to getting back to you after."

They'd both been amazed at how willingly a man would rendezvous with a woman he didn't know from Eve at the slightest hint of a little action, even with the Sex-Kitten Killer running amok.

She kissed Tamara and scooted her naked body next to her accomplice. "I'm so glad you're home safe."

"I read that most serials love the limelight. Love to read about what they've done and hear it on TV. They get off on it. That's one of the things that makes us different. Telling each other is enough. Tough love's a bitch sometimes."

"Tag. I'm it," Freda sighed.

\<work of art\>
Keith Gouveia

Peter had driven for an hour, searching the streets for a suitable partner. The thought of being alone and doing the job solo sickened him, but since his plan was to be the only one doing the killing, he figured he was obeying the rules. He also thought if he had an accomplice—a witness who could expose him—it would add a degree of difficulty to his final score.

Despite the demand for this competition and the site getting infiltrated by some punk kid, the little community was growing on him. Regardless of who won, Peter could not deny the fact that this was exactly what Mike needed to boost his confidence. He had always considered Mike to be the Lenny to his George, the mouse to his man.

The years of bullying were still evident in his friend. How many beatings had Mike endured because he was different from the others? Because his parents weren't wealthy? Or because he was there and didn't fight back?

Anger washed over Peter like a tidal wave crashing upon the shore as his mind tortured him with visions of Mike on his knees, begging for it to end.

"I need to kill one of them," he mumbled as he white-knuckled the steering wheel.

He continued to drive down the road until spotting a group of women with tall hair, painted faces, dressed in sequin skirts and faux furs draped over their shoulders. Behind them, a brunette leaned against the cinderblock wall with one leg propped against it, exposing a shapely thigh with a black garter.

Why isn't she with the others? he thought, then pulled up to the curb.

The group of women circled the passenger side door like ravenous wolves. Cleavage filled the open window as they demanded to be seen.

"Hey hun! Looking for a good time?"

"Ooh look at him ladies. One of us is in for a good time tonight."

Their chorused cackle did little to distract him from the heady scent of their combined perfume. The flowery aroma over-powered the years of musk accumulated in his Chevy Cavalier, and stung his nostrils. He fought against the urge to sneeze.

"I'm sure each of you lovely ladies could provide me with a wonderful time, but, I'm more interested in her." Peter pointed to the lone woman.

"She's not feelin' well, hun."

Peter narrowed his eyes to show he meant business and said, "Let me hear it from her."

"Okay," said the lead hooker before she turned around. "Sally, you're up!"

The other ladies spread out from the car mumbling incoherently as Sally sashayed her way toward the open passenger side window. She leaned in, head at an odd angle, and provocatively placed her elbows on the door frame so as to push her 'C' size breasts together. "You looking for a little company?"

She's hiding something. "Let me see your face."

"What for, hun? It's not like you'll be takin' your eyes off my tits."

Peter leaned toward her and grabbed her by the chin. With force he turned her face so she was looking square at him.

"Hey! Not so rough! That's extra."

"Who did this to you?" he asked, inspecting the purplish blotch around her left eye.

She stared at him flatly, all business now. "Still interested?"

"Yeah. Get in."

"How much we talkin'?"

"That depends on how dirty you're willing to get," he replied. "Get in."

Without argument, Sally opened the door and sat down.

Once the door was closed, Peter pulled away from the curb and said, "I can help you."

"No one can help me." She pulled away from him.

"I'm assuming it was your pimp. Am I right?"

She said nothing.

"I can see to it he never lays a hand on you again. All you have to do is point him out to me. I'll make it worth your while."

She thought for the slightest moment, and then nodded.

"Where to?"

"There's a motel right up the road. We have a room and Reverend Sneed is always there to check on us."

The car swerved slightly as Peter's neck snapped to the side. There was no smile on her face or twinkle in her eye to relay that she was joking. The name sounded ridiculous to his ear and it was one more reason to kill the stupid son-of-a-bitch.

"That's him," she said, her voice dull and flat. She pointed to a man in a white-fur coat propped against a neon-green Toyota Supra with aluminum sport rims, side skirts, and a spoiler—an obvious fan of the Fast and Furious franchise. A larger man stood with him, a no-neck, roid-rager dressed in "Tap-Out" clothing like an Ultimate Fighting billboard, obviously some sort of bodyguard or enforcer.

Peter looked away from the fool and noticed the woman's hands tightly squeezing her knees.

"It'll be all right," he said in a tone usually reserved for children. "No need to be nervous, I'll protect you."

She gave an insincere smile.

They pulled up to a long, white building with a blue carport extending out from the manager's office just big enough for two cars. The paint cracked and peeling and the neon L in the motel sign no longer working.

"What exactly is the plan?"

If Mike was here, the bodyguard would be no problem. "The plan's simple, really, and it all hinges on you. Once we're in the room, you'll go tell…" He couldn't bring himself to saying the cartoonish name. "…asshole to join us. That I like to watch. Make sure the bodyguard stays behind."

"Then what?"

"I put the fear of God in him and with this," Peter pulled out a wad of cash from his breast pocket. "You'll be able to go anywhere and start over again."

"I don't know if I can do it," she said, eyeing the money.

"Then I'll just have to find someone who can. I'm sure one of the—"

She snatched the money from his hand. "I'll do it!"

"Good."

"I'll just need to get the key and make sure the room is available."

"Okay," she said, her head bobbing up and down. Her eyes held a faraway look giving Peter the feeling she was going to flake on him.

"It's going to be all right," he said in the calmest and reassuring voice he could muster.

"I know. I'm just getting myself in the zone."

"That I understand. I usually get myself psyched—"

"No," she said, "this is different. Everything must be turned off. No emotions and no feeling whatsoever."

When she walked up to the Reverend Sneed, he slid his hand around her waist and roughly grabbed her ass. She looked uncomfortable and Peter could only imagine the deprived words rolling off the man's greasy tongue.

Filthy pig, Peter thought.

A brief conversation transpired before the pimp handed her a key. With the key in hand, she pointed to their room. Peter stepped out of his car and retrieved his duffle bag from the back seat before meeting her at their room door.

Peter pushed open the door and entered the room. A pungent odor bombarded Peter's nostrils, a mixture of feces and week old trash. A solid maroon bedspread covered the king size bed and he could only imagine the action it had seen, and the stains a black light would reveal. He dropped his duffle bag by the love seat, then walked through the room, noticing cigarette burns on the furniture and bedding. Upon entering the bathroom, he knew the place was the perfect setting. The white sink stained brown, a ring of fungi growing around the drain, and the mirror cracked and broken. It was apparent no one came around here, and those that did were nothing more than the dregs of society.

"How will I know you're ready?" she asked in a whisper.

"Give me a quick minute and I'll be ready."

He stole one last glance over his shoulder at Sally. Her head still bobbing and her lips moving as if she were chanting a mantra.

"You can do it," he told her, willing her some strength as she left, then closed the door behind her.

He gave all the door handles, light switches, and faucet handles a quick disinfecting wipe. Then set up his camera on its tripod and placed it behind the thick, maroon curtains of the right side window. When Sally brought his prey, he planned on playing it cool, sitting cross-legged in the chair with an air of mystery.

Peter had just settled in when he heard a strong, male voice just outside the door.

"Like hell you're going to stand out here and wait. You a pervert?"

"No boss. I—"

"I plan on getting my money's worth out of her. Get out there and check on the other girls. Make sure this isn't some kind of distraction to stiff me."

Awesome. Peter could not believe his luck and then felt ashamed for his use of the word. *Maybe I really am missing Mike,* he wondered, but had no time to dwell on it. Sally entered the room, her pimp a few steps behind, gaze fixated on her taught ass.

"Been too long since I tapped that," he said.

Decked out in fur and gold, the young white man looked to be having an identity crisis in Mike's eyes.

"So you're the perv?" he asked.

Peter nodded. *One less wannabe playa' in the world,* he thought as Sally sat down upon the bed and spread her legs.

"What's a matter, you don't speak English?"

"I speak just fine," Peter said, his right hand pressed to his chin. "Just pretend I'm not here."

With a shaking finger, the pimp said, "This is gonna cost ya."

"Whatever price you see fit."

With a smile, the pimp turned to Sally and just stood there staring down at her as if contemplating his first move.

Looking impatient, Sally stood up and pressed the palms of her hands against his chest, then kissed him softly on the lips.

Sneed pulled away from her embrace and pushed her down on the bed. She landed on her ass and barely bounced on the worn out mattress.

"Suck me," he said as he attacked his jewel encrusted belt buckle. "Then I'm going to fuck that ass." Sneed stole a quick glance at Peter and winked as if he knew what Peter wanted to see.

Sally gripped the half-erect cock and guided it between her lips, taking it all like she hadn't eaten in weeks.

"Damn girl."

My sentiments exactly, Peter thought as he rubbed against his own erection.

Watching drove Peter to the edge of orgasm, but before he could reach his climax, Reverend Sneed pulled Sally away and tossed her to the bed. He mounted her and the sight of his bare ass as he thrust in and out of her, caused Peter's erection to dissipate.

Ruined it!

As the asshole built toward his climax, his head rocketed upward with his eyes squinted, and Peter made his move.

He grabbed hold of the machete hidden behind the chair and approached the bed undetected with it raised above his head.

"Yeah, bitch!" Sneed exclaimed and then Peter slammed the blade into the side of the pimp's neck.

Blood splashed across Sally's back as the body fell to the left. The force of the blow sunk the blade halfway into his neck and caused the body to tumble off the bed.

Feeling the warm, crimson fluid upon her, Sally opened her eyes and turned to see Peter standing behind her. "What happened?" Her left hand reached behind her back.

Peter smiled as she wiped the blood away.

When she saw her blood-soaked hand, her eyes widened, her mouth gaped open, and a scream began to build. He acted fast; he covered her mouth, blocking her scream just before she released it.

"Shhhh! We don't want to alert anyone," he said, his voice calm and collected. "I'm going to take my hand away now."

"What did you do? How could you?"

"Now now. Let's not get hysterical. You wanted my help remember?"

"But... this isn't—"

"Doesn't matter. You're an accomplice now."

"Bullshit!"

"Sorry, sweetie, but that's how the cops are going to see it. And besides, that bodyguard of his never saw me, only you."

Tears pooled in her eyes as she looked down at the corpse. "If you were going to kill him, why'd you let him fuck me?"

"Yeah... sorry about that, I liked watching you." He shuffled his feet. "You're not mad, are you?"

"Mad? I'm fucking pissed!"

"Lower your voice," he said.

"As if," she said, running her hand through her disheveled hair—a poor attempt at collecting herself, he thought. "What now?"

"Glad you asked," he said, then turned toward the body.

He placed his right foot on the dead man's body, grabbed the machete, and pulled with all his might. A geyser of blood rushed out of the wound as the blade was freed.

"Ewe," Sally said as she turned away.

"Don't get disgusted yet. I just started."

Peter lifted the machete over his head again, but this time he targeted the man's left arm. With one fell swoop, the blade lodged itself into the shoulder. When the blood splashed upon his face, Sally turned to the right and heaved, spilling her stomach onto the brown, shag carpet.

"Light weight," he said, pulling the machete free again, and then delivered another blow. It took an additional blow to sever the arm from the torso, but with it off, Peter turned his attention to the other one. With that one severed, the head was his next target.

Sally could no longer tolerate the hacking and slashing, and ran into the bathroom, slamming the door behind her. Peter ignored her and continued to work. The head rolled several inches from the body on the second blow to the neck. He then rolled the decimated body onto its right side and, using the machete, he sliced the skin from the empty shoulder socket down to the hip. Carefully, he slid the blade under the skin and began to carve it off.

Nearly a half an hour passed by before Peter went into the bathroom after Sally. He found her perched on the toilet, knees pressed against her tits.

"You have a razor on you?"

"Yes," she said.

"I need one."

"For what?"

"Just give me one."

Sally rummaged through her purse and pulled out a pink, generic razor.

"Thank you," he said, taking it from her.

She followed him out of the bathroom. "Oh my God! What are doing?"

On the floor lay the young man's severed head and arms. The rest of his body was intact, except his chest and back: they were void of skin.

Turning to the left, she noticed the man's skin adorning the wall where Peter had stretched and tacked it.

A dry heave traveled over her lips.

"You all right?"

"NO! What the *fuck* is this?" she asked, pointing to the horrifying sight.

"That's my canvas," he simply replied.

"Canvas?"

"Yes. What did you expect me to use for my masterpiece? Paper?"

"I don't...." Her right hand shot up toward her temple. "The room... spinning." Sally waivered and her face was a mask of horror.

"Ahh," he said waving his hand, "you don't know anything about art. Any other canvas and my work is just as dull as everyone else's," Peter said as he walked up to the mounted piece of gore. He then began to shave the back hair off the tattered flesh with Sally's razor.

Sally planted herself on the bed, away from the body. Confusion, fear, and doubt prominently displayed on her face as Peter continued making passes with the razor.

Believing it was the sight of the skinless body that made her sick; Peter moved the body, pieces and all, to the tub.

"Care for a little head?" he asked, holding the severed head up, a feeble attempt at lightening the mood.

"You disgust me!" Sally snarled.

Peter's smile faded. He tossed the head into the bathroom and lurched toward her. "Then why don't you just leave!" he said, grabbing her by the arms and shaking her.

"You're hurting me—"

"Know this. If I get caught, I'm naming you as my accomplice."

"You wouldn't."

He laughed at her ignorance. "Wouldn't I?"

"Why are you doing this?"

"I'm in a little competition. Just a friendly game—"

"Friendly?"

"Yeah. So, are you leaving, or are you going to stick around and see what I paint?"

<shall we dance?>
Mark Onspaugh

The first death I arranged was actually an accident.

Oh, it doesn't say that in the brochure. My marketing expert thought it would be better if every murder I've been affiliated with was planned and executed without error.

I can see the wisdom in that, but we all benefit from what are called "happy accidents", life's little surprises.

When I was ten I was entered in our Cub Scout Pack's soapbox derby. This was a low-tech, non-electronic form of amusement where contestants build wooden go-carts and race downhill. Wii probably has a virtual version of it. At the time I was just six months from being old enough for Boy Scouts.

Anyway, this was one of those activities adults force children into to promote camaraderie and good sportsmanship. In those days there were no video games, not even ancient ones like Pong or Asteroids, so we were forced to build crappy little racers that only went fast because of gravity.

I had decided to call my racer the U.S.S. Enterprise, after the starship on Star Trek. I was a space nut and thought there was nobody cooler than Captain Kirk and Mr. Spock.

Trouble was, I told my friend Jimmy Connelly my intentions. He thought it was a great idea—so much so that he registered the name before I had a chance to.

I was as angry as a ten-year-old can get. Jimmy made things worse by saying I could name my ship the Galileo, after the Enterprise shuttlecraft.

Shuttlecraft, like he was the shark and I was the remora. Bastard.

I decided to teach Jimmy a lesson.

A soapbox racer essentially looks like an enclosed canoe on wheels. Since the cars are fairly long and the boys are fairly short, there is a lot of open space in the front and rear of the vehicle.

My older brother Mike was, at thirteen, the neighborhood dealer in fireworks, cigarettes and other contraband. He had never let me use any of his wares, but I knew where he stashed them.

I took a number of bottle rockets, roman candles and helicopters. Also in his stash was a box labeled "Genyuine (sic) M-80's". Having never been privy to the use of these (they were highly illegal and thus highly sought after by his clientele), I assumed these were of modest power and probably filled with confetti. I took these, some fuses, some wooden matches, sandpaper and the guts from two radio-controlled cars.

After bundling the fireworks into two groups with intertwined fuses, I hot glued sandpaper on one wheel of each RC car, then hot glued a match against the sandpaper. Once activated, the match would ignite and touch off the fuses of the fireworks. This would lead to a spectacular display and probably Jimmy Connelly wetting his pants.

Late that night, I snuck into the Connelly's garage. We were a small town, and no one felt the need to lock doors or secure such spaces.

I carefully duct taped each homemade bomb into the interior of Jimmy's Enterprise, one in the nose and one in the tail. By 3 p.m. tomorrow he'd be hitting warp speed.

I had a moment's hesitation as I was leaving the garage, then I saw how cool the words "U.S.S. Enterprise" looked on his racer, especially with authentic looking font and graphics. I left feeling happy and ready for the big day.

There were ten of us in that race. We all shook hands and smiled for our parents' cameras. I felt the comforting contours of the RC remote control in my pocket.

My very first detonator.

Jimmy's dad was an aerospace engineer and had given Jimmy's "ship" some extra loving care. This was against the rules, each boy was supposed to build his own car with minimal assistance. Too bad the old man wasn't along for the ride, I thought.

We got in our cars, and Jimmy pointed to the name on my racer, "The Invader".

"Nice," he said, with a smirk that meant he thought it was lame.

I just smiled and said, "Good luck."

He was about to offer some smartass rejoinder when the official called out, "On your marks, get set…"

The starter pistol went off and Jimmy shot forward like an actual rocket. In seconds he had a good ten feet on all of us, then fifteen.

I depressed the button on my remote, my heart hammering.

Nothing happened, and I almost panicked. I willed myself to act normal.

Suddenly, the front of Jimmy's car exploded, taking most of his legs with it. Multi-colored flames and sparks shot out the back end, and the spectators were showered with tiny slivers of balsa wood and Jimmy Connelly.

Jimmy's dad had used some pricey resin on his racer, and this turned out to be extremely flammable. The car transformed into a fireball that sped down Carver Street, roman candles and helicopters erupting from it like a multi-hued comet's tail. It crashed into the Carver Street Bakery and Jimmy's burning corpse smashed through the plate glass window and into a seven-tier wedding cake display. The boy looked like an overdone pig at a luau, and the street was filled with the smells of cordite, cooked pork and burnt sugar.

I puked when I saw what had become of my friend and rival, but was secretly proud of the conflagration I had caused.

I always did love surprises. I think everyone does.

And bad or tragic surprises make the best stories.

Jimmy's dad was blamed, everyone assuming the fireworks were stashed to be part of a victory lap, and the trauma of his son's fiery death drove him crazy, which only fueled the townspeople's assumptions of his guilt.

The thing is, Jimmy became famous. His story, "Kid Fireball" became a cautionary tale by fire departments across the country. It was the stuff of nightmares for many who witnessed it. It spawned several urban legends; none that I felt were as fantastic or grisly as the truth.

Even today, some forty years later, people in my home town still talk about it.

That's immortality.

I didn't have an urge or inclination to kill anyone else for several years, but Jimmy's status as a legend stuck with me. I was miserable in college, even though I had a natural aptitude for electronics and chemistry. The courses bored me, as did the pompous students and their oh-so important discussions and travails.

What to do?

The lure of criminal endeavors held more of a thrill for me, a challenge like booby-trapping that soapbox derby car so long ago.

I considered robbery, but it seemed very risky, even in the relatively low-tech 70s. I was not bound by conventional ethics or morality, but I did cherish my freedom.

I would not risk prison.

It occurred to me that I could provide a service no one else had thought of.

Oh, there have been plenty of ignominious and fantastic deaths, but these have rarely been planned or intended for the benefit of the victim.

My concept was two-fold: a fantastic death of an enemy would give a certain vicarious cachet to the perpetrator, and the grand death of a loved one could be both a celebratory act and a way to give them a kind of immortality.

Just as a car dealer needs at least one model on the showroom floor to do business, I needed a wondrous death to bring in clientele. Certainly something more recent than my Cub Scout "project".

His name was Ryan Devereaux. We lived on the same floor in the Dykstra Hall dorm at UCLA. I had fallen madly in love with a girl on our floor named Cheryl Matsumoto. She laughed at my jokes and was always playing with her hair or giving me playful hits, which were sure signs of attraction, according to my psych text.

I was shy, though, and kept waiting for the right opportunity. I casually mentioned her to Ryan, which seemed to open his eyes to the wonders of Cheryl Matsumoto.

Jesus, it was the U.S.S. Enterprise all over again.

By the time I had gotten up the nerve to ask Cheryl out, she and Ryan were an item. I had the horrible experience of hearing her loud moans of pleasure as I was about to knock on her door. I knew it was her because I had waited until her roommate was gone. I knew it was Ryan because I surreptitiously kept watch until he emerged from her room at just before dawn.

The rage I felt at ten was nothing like my rage at 19.

If Ryan died that would free up Cheryl Matsumoto and jumpstart my business.

In September I spent a week brainstorming Ryan's demise, and another six weeks planning it and getting the proper supplies.

Then I had to wait ten weeks. That was fine; it helped me cultivate patience, which is essential in my business.

On Thursday, January 1, 1976, Ryan Devereaux left his room at Dykstra Hall and proceeded southeast to Parking Structure 7. He was picking up Cheryl at her home and going to the Rose Bowl to watch the UCLA Bruins play the Ohio State Buckeyes.

His car was a 1973 Ford Mustang Fastback, black on blue.

I was waiting in the back seat.

Ryan was a jock, but few men expect someone in the back seat with a handkerchief full of chloroform.

He struggled briefly, but I had both the strength of vengeance and a Protestant work ethic on my side. I took pride in what I did, and did it well.

When Ryan was unconscious I dragged him out of the car. The parking structure was empty, most were either still on winter break or at the game. This gave me plenty of time to give Ryan a complete makeover.

Scandal was an essential part of my vengeance, and my business plan.

I put Ryan in the passenger seat and drove across the deserted campus to Ackerman Union and Joe.

It was a big year for UCLA, what with being in the Rose Bowl for the bicentennial and all. The administration had gone all out, even bringing a large brown bear from the L.A. Zoo to serve as mascot during Spirit Week. The bear was guarded at all times and was slated to go home the following day.

The guard always had a thermos of coffee with him, and always took a bathroom break at noon, figuring the bear—whom the students had nicknamed "Joe Bruin"—would be safe during that five minutes.

That was plenty of time for me to drug his coffee prior to "picking up" Ryan.

The guard was sleeping peacefully when we arrived. I parked near Joe's cage. I wanted it to look as if Ryan had driven himself there. I was wearing gloves and had no worries about being identified. I had taken the precaution of wearing lifts, a blonde wig and dark glasses, just on the off chance I was spotted.

I dragged Ryan over to the bear's cage.

Using the guard's key I opened the cage. I put Ryan in and the bear regarded him with little interest as I locked the cage.

I had expected this. Joe had been raised in the zoo and was used to keepers and custodians, not to mention thousands of visitors calling to him and making faces and snapping pictures.

I had a way to get him in touch with his more wild nature, but first I wanted Ryan awake for what was to come. Not so much to make him suffer (although that would be a happy bonus) as him being awake was essential to my plan.

I retrieved my "bear persuader" from the car, then reached through the bars and broke an ammonia capsule under Ryan's nose. I placed the fragments in a bag as Ryan came around.

He saw me, then registered his "makeover".

"What... what the hell is this?"

"Goodbye," I said, smiling.

A cattle prod delivers some 5,000 volts. If held in place long enough, it can sear and blister the skin, even the skin of a tough, heavily furred bear.

One zap from the prod was enough to remind Joe Bruin that he was a savage animal and that a human had invaded his space.

As the bear charged, Ryan didn't play dead. He panicked, which only made the injured bear more enraged.

As Joe Bruin was removing most of Ryan's left arm, I unlocked the padlock and left the keys on the ground.

I left with the prod and a bag containing the chloroform, rag and ammonia capsule.

Ryan's screams were enough to rouse the guard, who thought a cheerleader was being torn apart by the usually docile brown bear. The bear was in such a frenzy the guard could do nothing but radio for help.

By noon the following day the story of Ryan's bizarre death was the stuff of legend. Why was Ryan dressed like a cheerleader, wearing even women's underwear and makeup? Was it a prank gone wrong? A fraternity hazing? Had he been insane?

Ryan's demise was deemed "death by misadventure", although some called it "suicide by bear". Several wags were able to make off-color puns involving drag queens and Boo Boo Bear. Ryan's family wanted Joe Bruin put to death, but animal rights activists and most of the UCLA student body agreed that Ryan had provoked the poor creature, and Joe was able to return to his grotto at the L.A. Zoo.

Visitors to his cage increased by 33%, and no one threw anything at him.

I named my company Danse Macabre and had some spiffy business cards made up. Nowadays it's fairly easy to set up special email accounts and encrypt them, then bounce them off several servers on a rotating matrix. Back in the 70s I had to use coded personal ads and P.O. boxes. Very primitive, but effective, if you were careful.

I also kept the tools of my new trade in a couple of storage lockers in Culver City. Anyone searching my dorm room would only find the property of a gifted, committed student.

That was a bonus of offing Ryan. Now that I had a real career, my school work was a joy. It was now like playing a part, the part of a good student without any violent tendencies.

I gave Cheryl time to get over Ryan's grisly death,

then asked her out. Danse Macabre gave me a newfound confidence that she found appealing.

I had one serious rival for Cheryl's affection, and that was Lee, an art major looking to become an animator. I fattened my resume with Lee's death. He was found in a restroom stall, most of his face blown off from an exploding cigar. Unlike the CIA and their failure with Castro, my stunt was colorful and legendary. Cigar sales in Westwood fell by 20% for a full two months.

Over the years I provided both nobodies and celebrities with the sort of death that would never leave the public consciousness. Long after their life's work has been forgotten or trivialized, their death would still be told in bars, at parties and around campfires.

The chemistry professor who ingested liquid nitrogen instead of his Snapple Peach-Flavored Ice Tea. Witnesses say he shattered before the bottle did when it hit the floor.

The deli owner killed by his own slicer. The client on that one had a grudge against the owner and his whole family, so the cold cuts served at the wake were, shall we say, his "personal best".

The Egyptologist found mummified inside his wedding cake. It was a good cake, too, a Cuban Tres Leches cake. I was there as a photographer and was the only one who felt like having a piece.

The director who specialized in slasher films. His death was a "greatest hits" of his last five films and involved stabbing, sawing, acid, arrows, a morning-star, gunshot, power sander, cockroaches, fire, poison, leeches, piranha and decapitation by a pendulum like the one in Poe's story. The challenge was for all 13 to take place simultaneously during his birthday party. The client on this was actually a group of rival directors. They not only paid me, but gave me a "director's cut" of the murder(s).

The newspaper magnate who, foreseeing the death of

print by electronic media, elected to be killed by his own presses. Copies of that day's headlines in his blood and ink sold for thousands on eBay.

The gold medal swimmer killed by a great white shark in his backyard pool.

The fitness guru who had scammed hundreds with phony weight loss pills. An obsessive vitamin junkie, he ingested several gel capsules containing white phosphorous. Once activated most of him burned away as his girlfriend looked on in horror. To this day I have people swear to me it was a documented case of spontaneous human combustion.

The hotel heiress whose best friend and rival had her devoured by a pack of Chihuahuas in Tiffany collars.

The comic book writer who dressed like a caped hero and "jumped" out of a commercial airliner over Manhattan. That was an unpleasant surprise for the kids of P.S. 6 when he landed on the playground at lunch.

My brother Mike, whose wife got tired of his constant affairs. She contacted Danse Macabre having no idea it was my company. Since they were family, I gave her a big discount and Mike a most spectacular death. You've heard of the "Spider Guy", the one who was on the subway when hundreds of black widows erupted from every orifice in his body? That was my big brother. Graffiti artists still paint an homage to him.

Over the years I have engineered some two hundred spectacular or ironic deaths. In that time I married Cheryl and we raised a son and daughter, Edward and Charlotte, both now in their thirties with families of their own.

Danse Macabre has branch offices in Rio de Janeiro, Paris, Madrid, Berlin, Tokyo, New Delhi and Cairo. Within five years we'll have offices in Dubai, Stockholm, Beijing, Sydney and Johannesburg. I also expect to open offices in Ottawa, Vietnam, Thailand, Ukraine and one of the Koreas within ten years.

Death is good business.

But it's not just the money.

It's the challenge, *the fun*.

Now I am en route to my 70th birthday party. It's being held at the home of a friend in the Hamptons, one of my oldest and most frequent clients.

The party is supposed to be a surprise, and I haven't told anyone I know.

I also know that Cheryl, Edward and Charlotte have planned a spectacular death for me. When you've been in the business for some forty years you get a feel for these things.

Oh, I could have figured out what they were up to, even thwarted it… But what fun would that be? I'm slowing down, and it's getting more and more difficult to keep up with my kids and grandkids.

Besides, do I want to die slipping in the bathtub or in a hospital bed with tubes in my nose?

Please.

So I'll go, a happy little lamb to a spectacular slaughter.

I always did love a surprise.

<TO the victor Goes the spoils>

Keith Gouveia

"Well that was an odd post," said Mike as Peter clicked a hyperlink away from the message board.

"I know, right? But, we've got an odd bunch here."

"You think it's true about his company? You think his family really would kill him?"

Peter gave his friend a sideways glance. "Danse Macabre isn't something you can Google, but yeah, it's the real deal. And as to whether or not they killed him...." He thought on it for a moment and then finally shrugged his shoulders.

"Kind of wish we were here for him."

Peter placed a hand on his friend's shoulder and said, "I doubt it would have made a difference."

Mike nodded. "Probably right. Anyway, we've delayed this long enough. As promised, I didn't fiddle with your precious computers." Mike ejected the memory card from the digital camera and handed it to him.

Peter tried his best to fight the smile forcing its way across his cheeks. Surely Mike's snapshots were no comparison to the video footage he had recorded. *Round one goes to me,* he thought as he plucked the small card from Mike's fingers.

"That smug look is unbecoming."

"C'mon, Mike, it's all in fun."

"We'll see how much fun you're having after I cutoff that pinky of yours."

Peter could feel the smile on his face. He inserted the memory card in his computer and uploaded the images.

As the files opened, Peter's eyes went wide at the horrifically beautiful snapshots displayed. *He did this?* He swallowed hard at the thought.

"What do you think?" Mike asked, wide-eyed and still.

"I'm... impressed."

A wide grin stretched across Mike's face and his fists balled in excitement. "Damn right you're impressed."

"Settle down," Peter said, turning his attention back to the digital photos of three decapitated heads placed atop a fireplace mantle, their severed hands nailed in position to reflect Peter's favorite sculpture. The patriarch's hands covered his eyes, the matriarch's covered her ears, and the little boy's overlapped his mouth. *See no evil, hear no evil, speak no evil... it's brilliant,* Peter thought.

"You're scared."

"Mike, if you don't shut up, I'm going to smack that shit-eating grin right off your face."

"Ah," he said with the wave of his hand, "you're just jealous."

"I think it's time I showed you *real* art."

Peter had already uploaded his video to the forum, and by the time he brought the web page up for Mike, there were fifteen comments.

"No fair!"

"What?" he asked, but knew full well what Mike was complaining about.

"You got a jump on me."

"Nothing new there, my friend. Now watch."

With the click of his mouse, the small pixilated screen came alive with Sally ushering in his victim. Mike slouched over and watched with unblinking eyes as Sally performed.

"Where'd you find her?" Mike asked, his right hand nonchalantly disappearing into his right-front pocket.

"On the street," he answered.

"Did you kill her?"

"Just keep watching."

As Mike continued to watch the video, Peter's gaze traveled down to the first response.

What does Mrdrman1968 have to say? he wondered, then read the paragraph.

Son of a bitch, he thought as he leaned back into his chair. His gaze traveled to the next comment left by SlayMeB4IU, but half of its text disappeared beyond the computer screen window. However, he got the gist of the message from what was visible. *How can they accuse me of cheating?*

"What's that smile for?" Peter asked.

Mike pointed to the screen and said, "You were thinking about me. That proves it."

Peter stared at his creation. The portrait of the dead dog the two had happened upon all those years ago betrayed him, an undeniable tell-tale sign of his true emotions. "You're reading too much into it," he said with a nonchalant wave of his hand. "I just wanted something bloody."

"We've killed how many people? And yet you still choose the dog. Don't get me wrong," Mike said, palms up, "it's your most beautiful painting to date, and I'm flattered."

"It was a metaphor. The guy was a pimp. A dog. Now he's a dead dog," Peter said, "but you're still…what are you doing?"

Mike leaned in and wrapped his arms around him. The display of affection catching Peter off guard.

"Seriously?" Peter asked, then accepted it and gave a single, one-handed pat on Mike's back. "Can we get back to the task at hand?"

"Sure," Mike broke away. "It's too bad I can't hang that in my room. The blood…I remember it vividly. Even after all these years you captured every nuance." Mike's hand reached for the monitor. "The blotches of blood and tangled fur, the terrible crook in its neck and lifeless tongue, the burst intestines…"

"Mike!" Peter said as his friend drew closer to the monitor as if he were dunking his head into a pool of water. "My screen."

"Right," he said, straightening his back. "Sorry, got lost in the moment."

Peter nodded, and with one last sideways glance to make sure Mike was composed, he then dragged the scroll bar to reveal more messages.

"Why are they all accusing you of cheating and not being able to do it alone?" Mike asked. "Having a witness adds to the degree of difficulty."

"Exactly," he said with a smile. Peter was surprised to hear Mike's words. He took comfort in knowing that regardless of what the simpletons on the message board thought, his best bud understood and "got it".

Mike pointed to the left side menu bar. "It looks like my photos are getting replies."

"Let's see what they say," Peter replied as he rolled the thumb ball of his mouse. He clicked the corresponding hyperlink and the page refreshed. "Sonuvabitch," he mumbled.

Mike leaned in closer to read the messages and when he straightened his back, the smile stretched across his face caused Peter's stomach to clench.

"Looks like I've got CutThroat's and Hitman007's votes." Mike crossed his arms in front of his chest as if victory was his.

"It's still early, my friend." Peter returned his gaze to the computer screen and watched as the votes rolled in.

As the minutes passed, Peter nervously bit his bottom lip. He peeled strips of skin, one after another, and when he tasted blood, he turned his attention to his upper lip. With each vote Peter got, Mike received two or three and it wasn't before long he knew the lead was too great to overcome. But being the true friend he was, Mike said nothing until the final vote was cast.

"Look, maybe we shouldn't—"

"Nonsense," Peter said, "a bet's a bet. You won."

"We don't have to do it tonight, with the party and all."

"Thank you," Peter said.

"But I'm sure the guys would want to watch, we could—"

"No! I don't want them to see me pass out."

"They'd love that," Mike said.

"Is your bag ready?"

"Yeah, but…"

"What is it?" Peter asked.

"Don't you think this goes against everything we've stood for?"

"That's why I'm not taking the reins on this one. Besides, we may walk away with a future target after tonight."

Mike smiled at the prospect.

\<NSFW\>

Lorne Dixon

Getting Joel to abandon the idea that they should wear a clown suit into the church was like dragging a preschooler away from a fast-food jungle gym. Curtis had to explain in careful, thoughtful words, that killing a priest during midnight mass wearing face paint and red size twenty shoes would inevitably lead news reports later to blame the Insane Clown Posse for the crime. Curtis knew Joel hated that band and would detest the idea of them getting any of the credit. So, finally, Joel agreed on black trench coats.

"K and H style," Curtis said. The letters stood for *Klebold and Harris*. He took his hands off the steering wheel long enough to reach across to the passenger seat and give Joel a high-five. On the way back, his hand struck the pair of convenience store fountain drink cups in the center console, nearly spilling them.

"Jesus, man, be careful. You spill Code Red in here and your mom'll never let you borrow her wheels again." Joel reached down to the radio and flicked through the channels. "I can't believe that your iPod batteries died. Now we're stuck with—what is this, Nickelback?"

"Shinedown," Curtis corrected.

They both laughed. Jock music. Normally, they'd cruise the streets of Greater Valley listening to some obscure death metal band from Norway with a name neither of them could pronounce. Curtis found plenty of music online. He couldn't say he was a fan of any of them, really, he was more of a classic rock guy, but he enjoyed the stares from pedestrians when they pulled up to a stop light with the stereo blaring, offended faces full of anger and repulsion. Shinedown just didn't have the same effect.

"You know what, man?" Joel said, abandoning the radio. "Maybe we're thinking about this all wrong, got our wiring all twisted up. What if we wait for the service to end and wait outside? Father Roselle comes out and *bang*, get me? Right in the chest."

"No, dude." Curtis shook his head. "That shit reminds me of Mark David Chapman."

Joel's brow dropped. "And what's wrong with that?"

"Fuck that guy. Because of him, McCartney's gonna be the last Beatle. If he'd had the good sense to take out Paul we wouldn't have'ta hear none of that *Hope of Deliverance* shit." Turning off Main Street, Curtis jerked the wheel hard and screeched his mom's SUV into a parking spot along Bellamy Road. He killed the ignition and pocketed the keys right away. He had a bad habit of locking himself out.

"There's always Ringo," Joel said, releasing his seatbelt.

"Ringo? You gotta be shittin' me." Curtis shook his head and sputtered his lips as if shaking off a chill. "Anyway, it doesn't matter right now. We still got four months to Christmas, plenty of time to refine our plan."

Joel pointed down the street at the last house on the block. "That it?"

Nodding, Curtis wrenched up the parking brake. "Yeah. That's his place all right. I staked it out yesterday for a couple hours after school. Saw him come out with a bag of garbage, drop it at the curb, then walk his dog. I waited until he was down on Nelson Street before I rummaged through his trash."

"Find anything?" Joel asked. "Chips of bone, severed fingers, anything?"

"Mostly TV dinners and empty Bud cans."

"Salisbury steak?" Joel held his breath for the answer.

Curtis waved a hand. "Turkey and stuffing, and that weird ass cranberry glob in the corner."

Joel's brow lowered. "You sure this guy's the real deal, dude? I mean, you and I both know that the only TV dinner worth throwing down the gullet is Salisbury steak. You sure this guy's not..."

"Not *what?*" Curtis snickered.

"Well, y'know, maybe he's just, *gay* or something."

Curtis laughed. "No, man, he ain't like that. I've read his posts online for months and chatted with him on IM. He's cool. Where'd you get the idea that—"

"Fuck off... you laughing at me? I just remember, like, that German guy that took out that ad for someone to eat. When that stupid shit responded and came over, they like, did gay stuff beforehand—"

"You need to cut down on the Dew." Curtis opened the driver's side door and slid out onto the street. The sun was setting behind the peaked rooftops along Bellamy. Intense orange sunlight blasted their faces as they trotted down the sidewalk. Joel plucked a pair of Dolce & Gabanna sunglasses out of his hoodie's inside pocket and slapped them onto his face. Curtis gasped.

"What?" Joel asked with an annoyed lilt to his voice. "They're a birthday gift from my grandma."

Curtis shook his head and kept walking.

Embarrassed, Joel pocketed the shades.

Climbing a short set of concrete steps, they bounced up to the porch door. They exchanged a long stare, at first full of machismo and certainty, but quickly dissolving into queasiness and jangling nerves. It reminded Curtis of the time when, at fourteen, they'd pooled their allowances and lawn-cutting money with the goal of hiring a prostitute from the want ads in the back of the alternative weekly newspaper. Eventually, they'd spooked themselves enough to abandon the idea and buy a Playstation console instead. "Last exit, dude. Either we knock on the door or we hightail it to the Mall for raspberry mocha lattes."

For a moment Curtis was sure Joel was ready to back away from the door and agree to another night at the Starbucks, getting high on caffeine and staring at the girls entering and leaving the Hot Topic across the hall. But then a jack-o-lantern grin spread across his face and he rapped on the door.

"We're really doing this," he said.

Curtis flashed his eyes down the street. There were no unmarked white vans staking out the street. No faces peering out from behind pulled drapes. Hopefully, no one would remember they were ever here.

"Sure he's home?" Joel asked, a flicker of worry in his eyes.

Curtis nodded. "Talked to him last night on IM. He said he'll be here."

They waited another minute. Shrugging, Joel knocked again.

The door opened, startling them, and they stepped back, both almost losing their balance and tumbling down the porch steps. A disheveled man in a faded pink robe stood in the doorway, hair sticking out at wild angles, eyes bleary.

"Mrdrman1968?" Joel asked.

"Oh, right," he said, combing a hand through his hair. "You're the kids, right? Yeah. Sorry, I was napping. Had to work the late shift and...hey, come on in, come in."

Mrderman1968 stepped aside. Joel shot a look over to Curtis. If a glance could whisper, this one would ask, *you sure he's not into any gay stuff, right?*

Joel dropped a hand on his friend's shoulder, reassuring

him. He wondered why Joel was so worried about all that stuff. He seemed to mention homosexuals *constantly. Such a spaz.*

Stepping into the house, Curtis motioned for Joel to follow and he did, never straying more than a couple steps behind. It was a good enough example of their lives together. Growing up, Joel was always the kid to get into a fight he couldn't possibly win and Curtis was the one to see him through. Joel could knock on a door, but it was always Curtis who led the way.

The house seemed cluttered but normal, a living room with a threadbare recliner in its center facing an entertainment unit piled high with DVDs. To his surprise, most of the films were romantic comedies and tearjerkers. "You a big movie fan, Mrdrman1968?"

"Oh, hey, so maybe you just call me Stan, okay?" Stan said, motioning for them to take a seat on a poorly reupholstered loveseat. "I just use that name online, just 'cause you can't really use your real name. Y'know? You boys want a drink?"

They were teenagers—*of course* they wanted a drink. Stan disappeared into the kitchen for a moment before emerging with a half full bottle of Zinfandel and two plastic cups. He filled the cups, passing the bottle's mouth from one to the other without concern for the spillage, and handed them over. Then he took a swig from the bottle. "Sorry, the only thing in the fridge is wine."

Curtis wrinkled his nose. He supposed he should have been worried that Stan had coated the bottom of the cups with GHB or Rohypnol and Joel's worst fears would be realized, but he was more worried about backwash in the bottle. Still, it was no time to be an ungrateful guest, so he tipped back the cup and drank. Joel followed suit. As always.

"So, whatcha got in mind for tonight?" Stan asked. He

set the bottle down on the old Zenith cabinet television and dropped into his recliner. The chair made a sound like a mouse being crushed to death.

Joel sunk into the loveseat's cushions, the same way he would shrink away in class when the teacher was looking for the answer to a math equation. Curtis leaned forward, elbows on knees, and said, "Nothing in particular. We're new to all this and thought maybe you could just show us the ropes."

"No," Stan said. "Never use ropes. Too easy for the cops to trace the fiber. Stick with plastic zip ties and duct tape."

The tension left the room as an enormous smile bloomed on Stan's face. Curtis and Joel laughed. It was as if an eighty pound weight had been removed from their chests.

"Okay, sure, I'll show you how it's done," Stan said as he reached for the bottle. "Just one more drink first. To take the edge off. You guys want?"

Yes they wanted more wine. But not more backwash. They shook their heads *no*. Stan didn't seem disappointed. Instead, he tipped the bottle back against his lips, reclined his head back, and gulped down the last of the wine. Then he belched and pointed to the door. "Okay, then, hand me your keys. We're going on a class trip."

"Uh, we thought," Curtis stammered. "It's just that—"

"A problem?" Stan said, taking a step toward them. He held the wine bottle by its neck, like a short cudgel, and tapped it against his palm. "What's wrong?"

"You've been drinking. Do you think it's okay to drive?" Joel slid behind Curtis' shoulder as he spoke. "I mean, how much have you had tonight?"

Stan grinned. "I'm fine. Now, keys."

Curtis slid a hand down into the pockets of his jeans and fished around. His hands were shaking and numbing over. The key ring kept sliding out of his grasp.

"Playing with yourself or something?" Stan teased.

"No... I... uh," he said as he finally brought up the keys. Handing them over, he shivered. "It's my mom's Lexus. She was gonna get the Sequoia, but this gets better highway fuel mileage and she's all green and everything and it's a hybrid and—"

"Calm down," Stan said. It sounded more like a command than a request. Snatching up the key ring, he gave them a quick once over and spread the keys out with his thumb. Then he glanced at his wristwatch as he shrugged off the robe and let it drop to the floor. He wore blue jeans and a white beater underneath. The shirt bulged at his midsection. "I'll take good care of your mom's car. Her *hybrid* car. Now come on, the hands on the clock say it's time to rock."

Stan started for the door. Curtis followed, but for once Joel stayed glued in place. Glancing back, he asked, "What's up, man, com'mon, time to go."

Joel looked uncomfortable. "Gotta piss."

Stan, overhearing, pointed to the stairs. "Bathroom's right where you'd expect it, up the stairs, end of the hall. Hurry up. I can already feel my blood-alcohol level dropping, I don't want to do this thing sober."

"Come with me?" Joel asked. His eyes filled with sheepish, dilated pupils.

Curtis nodded. "Sure."

Stan rolled his eyes. "Just make it quick, ladies."

They hurried upstairs. Once out of Stan's view, however, they slowed down and crept down the hallway. They exchanged stares. Nothing was said, not with lips and tongues and vocal chords, but the look that passed between them was a conversation in itself:

"Maybe this wasn't a good idea."
"You think, Sherlock? I just want to get outta here."
"Dude, we can't just run off. He'll come after us."
"We're so fucked."

"So, so fucked."

They stopped at the bathroom door. Joel headed inside. "You'll, y'know, watch the door and stuff?"

"Sure," Curtis agreed.

Joel closed the door most of the way, leaving only a crack open. Curtis listened as his friend fumbled for the light switch. Then there was the sound of a porcelain toilet seat clanking against the tank. A full minute of silence. Then a steady drizzle of urine splashing into the bowl. Curtis kept his eyes on the stairs at the end of the hall, expecting Stan to come bounding up, eyes full of fire, a machete in both hands. But that didn't happen. Instead, the trickle of Joel's piss was interrupted by a volley of obscenities.

"You okay?" he called into the bathroom.

Clothes rustled. A zipper closed. "Curt, man, get in here."

Opening the door, he rushed inside and collided with Joel, who was quickly stepping away from the toilet. Joel pointed at the shower curtain. "In there."

"What is it?" he whispered.

"Just look."

"Hell no, just tell me."

Joel shook his head. "I'm kinda hoping that you pull back the curtain and there's nothing there, like maybe it was my imagination or something."

Curtis reached out for the shower curtain. Pulling it back, he thought of Janet Leigh—but not Anne Heche, *never* Anne Heche. Then, looking down into the blood-streaked tub, he forgot how to breathe for a while.

An old woman was crumbled on the porcelain, her head attached only by an exposed section of spine, a foot long hunting knife protruding from her right eye. Her walker rested on top of her.

"Shit," Curtis repeated.

Joel agreed. "Yeah, shit."

Shit seemed to be the only word they could conjure, so they put it to good use, each repeating it until it became a mantra, some kind of magical spell that they hoped would make the body disappear, or better yet, transport them out of the bathroom and into their regular chairs at Starbucks. They would have been ogling varsity cheerleaders in miniskirts instead of an old lady cut to pieces.

"This is so bad," Curtis said, although another *shit* probably could have conveyed the same idea. "I didn't think…I mean, it all looks so cool on television and in the movies."

"This ain't like that," Joel chirped.

"What do we do? He has my mom's keys."

Joel raised a fist. "Maybe we can take him?"

Curtis cocked a thumb back at the shower. "Dude, no, I don't think the two of us can take him. You see what he did to that old lady? It ain't gonna be like rolling freshmen for lunch money."

"Okay," Joel stretched out the word like the wiggling final note in the music of a spaghetti western: *ohhh-hhhhhhhh-kayyyyy-yyyyy-yyyy*. "So what'da we do?"

Stepping back into the hall, he said, "We go along with Stan for now, pretend like we're still cool with everything, and when we get the chance, put as much distance between us and him as possible."

Stan's voice called from the bottom of the stairs, "What're the two of you doing up there, handstands and hand jobs?"

As if responding to the bark of a drill sergeant, they scampered downstairs. Stan was waiting by the landing with a large folding hunting knife in his hands. The tip of his finger skated down the serrated blade, testing the edge. "Cut the outer skin without even applying any pressure. That's what you want every time. Always check your tools before you hit the road, boys."

Stan hadn't changed at all in the few minutes they'd been upstairs—hair still mussed, eyes still tired—but now he appeared to them as a completely different animal, no longer human at all, but something either more or less evolved, a dangerous splinter of the family tree Homo sapiens. Sliding the knife under his belt, he asked, "Anything catch your eyes up there?"

"No," they responded in one voice.

"Should have." His eyes flickered between the two teenagers. "Didn't see the dead bitch in the shower? There's another lesson for you, too: can't never judge who'll put up a fight or not. That old crow just didn't give up until the blood loss sapped her strength."

"Where'd you get her?" Joel asked, his voice shaking and barely louder than a whisper.

"Right here." Stan slapped the front door. "I knocked, she answered, I slid the blade under her chin and came on in. That was a week ago. She has satellite TV, the entire package, even porn. So I thought I'd stay for a while."

Curtis' eyes widened. "This is *her* house?"

"Do you really think I'd arrange to meet a couple of kids I don't know at *my* house?" He opened the door, held it, and gestured for Curtis and Stan to exit. "Do you suppose that a guy like me would stay in business for long if I took chances like that?"

Following Curtis, Joel stepped out of the house and asked, "I thought deep down everyone wants to be caught."

Stan stepped out and closed the door. "No, not really."

Stan led them to the Lexus. He didn't seem particularly concerned about being seen by the neighbors. As if reading Curtis' mind, he chuckled. "People only remember things when they know in advance that they should be paying attention. Everyone's too preoccupied these days to even notice a stranger on the street. The brain can only store so much. PTO meetings, dentist appointments, the expiration date on the milk in the fridge: all these things make me invisible."

Across the street, an old man came out of his front door, checked the mailbox nailed to his stoop, and waved to Stan.

Stan waved back and mumbled, "He won't remember this at all."

They piled into the SUV.

There wasn't much conversation during the forty-five minute drive. Occasionally, Stan would point out a landmark, but fail to explain its meaning to him: "tackle shop", "daycare center", "gym". Curtis wondered if these were all crime scenes. He tried not to guess what mental images were flickering through Stan's head. As the landscape transformed from residential to urban, Stan pointed out a tall, soot-black cinderblock building and grinned. "Factory."

"See how quiet it is out here? Fifteen years ago, would'a been people all over the place, but the jobs moved out and so did everyone who had pocket change to buy a bus ticket," Stan explained. "Cops stay on the other side of the city, out where there are still people and donut shops."

Finally, after winding through four desolate blocks, they saw an old black woman walking the cracked sidewalk. Bundled up in thrift store clothes and an oversized hair wrap, she reminded Curtis of history class videos about the Great Depression.

"Forget her," Stan said and kept driving.

Joel leaned in from the back seat. "What's wrong with her?"

"Keep it in your own race. I learned that a long time back. Did this Haitian kid who sold newspapers. Day after they found his body, all the papers started calling it a *hate crime*. Can you imagine that? *Hate* has nothing to do with it."

Six more blocks and it was beginning to look like finding a white victim was worse than the needle and haystack equation. On these empty streets, there wasn't even a haystack to comb through, just a spare stalk of dried hay scattered here and there: the occasional drifter or homeless vet. Stan dismissed each with the same wrinkle of his nose and shake of his head.

Then she appeared, sauntering out of a boarded up tenement apartment complex in a black miniskirt and white button-down tank top. Curtis guessed she was in her late twenties, although it was difficult to tell, stress lines and heavy makeup obfuscated any easy indication—he would have believed nineteen or forty-five.

"She looks just like, Mrs. Waldroff," Joel said.

Curtis spun in his seat. "She does *not* look like Mrs. Waldroff."

"Sure she does," Joel insisted. "Look at her."

"Who's Mrs. Waldroff?" Stan asked.

Curtis shook his head and turned away from Joel. "In fifth grade we had a substitute teacher for a couple months when Mr. Kirkland had a heart attack. Joel had the biggest crush on her."

"And she looked like this?" Stan asked, thumb pointing to the street walker. Curtis couldn't tell if the expression on his face was amusement or disappointment.

"Yes," Joel said enthusiastically.

"No," Curtis blurted out. "Not at all."

Stan pulled the Lexus to the curb and killed the engine. Then he pocketed the keys. "Okay, then, Mrs. Waldroff it is. The first one's always easier if you imagine someone you know anyway."

The SUV's heavy door swung shut and for a moment, Curtis and Joel were alone and outside Stan's earshot. Not letting the moment of privacy go to waste, Curtis twisted the rear view mirror and stared at his friend's pale face. "What are we doing, man? How is it that we're even here?"

"I dunno, you found this guy."

"I know, but, like, you always wanted to talk about serial killers and everything. You seemed so into it all—"

"—No, dude, don't push this off on me."

"Oh, come on, Joel, you were *so* excited. You told me to—"

"—I just...it was our thing, you know, talking about it. Something that we did, just you and I. It was something that our parents and all those assholes at school couldn't belittle or—"

Stan rapped knuckles on the passenger side window.

They let out moist sighs. "You ready?"

"Hell no."

Curtis opened the door and climbed out. Joel, ever reliable, slinked up between the seats and tumbled out behind him. Stan raised two fingers and pointed at their eyes. "Keep your head down as we walk. It's damn near impossible to tell where someone's looking when their face is pointing to the sidewalk. We get close, she'll start to walk faster. That's okay. Pick up your pace, but stay the same distance behind her. It'll unnerve her, but she won't be able to tell whether we're really following her or not."

Stan dropped his fingers and turned. Mrs. Waldroff was just reaching the end of the block and stepping out into the crosswalk. Heads down, they followed her across the deserted city blocks, passing windows repaired by duct tape and cardboard, stepping over a fallen parking meter. She turned a corner under an illegible street sign and continued through a corridor of condemned brick stones and public works duplexes. Night was falling and Curtis feared that without working streetlights—he hadn't seen a single one intact—they would lose her to the shadows. Mostly, he hoped she would disappear and Stan would give up, but then there was the question of what a frustrated psychotic might decide upon as the evening's consolation prize. He squinted and kept her in his sights.

Summer would be over soon. The scent of Autumn was already in the air, crisp leaves and ozone, buoyant in Curtis' lungs, the heavy humidity of August giving way to brisk mountaintop breezes. Senior year would follow and the tormentors would come out, beach tans fading, with stories of summer homes and trips to the islands, jeering with professionally whitened teeth and pointing with manicured fingernails.

On the last day of their Junior year, Joel had made him promise that they wouldn't stick around for another year of insults and threats. "We can just go, take your mom's car and go, get away from all this shit, leave all those assholes behind. No one's gonna miss us anyway, they're never gonna ask, *what happened to those two weird guys?* We could just be gone, man, disappeared and forgotten."

Curtis had promised.

Then, unexpectedly, Joel had hugged him.

As summer progressed, the talk changed from running away to shooting up the school on the first day of school. Then, with only days left before the school year began, the plan changed—they'd attack the homecoming dance in October. Then, a few days later, it was Christmas Mass. Curtis had no doubt that the massacre would have been postponed again—the prom, graduation—until Senior year was over and they began searching for jobs. Sure, they'd built a few pipe bombs. But they'd done that every summer since third grade.

Then he'd found the website.

Which, Curtis supposed, made it all his fault.

Stan's foot hit the door and old wood cracked and splintered, the deadbolt's cylinder broke free and a chain lock jangled as its foundation plate's screws uprooted from their holes. The floor burst in. Stan rushed through, knife flashing in his hands, and the boys froze. Inside, out of sight, Mrs. Waldroff screamed. It wasn't the precise, perfectly pitched scream of an actress in a slick Hollywood production, but an uneven, warbling sound belted out from a throat ravaged by alcohol and nicotine.

Staring down the hallway. *How many of these shithole apartments are occupied,* Curtis wondered as his eyes passed from door to door, from graffiti to chipped molding, from the nicks of knives and the dents of fists. Would any of them hear Mrs. Woldroff's scream and come to their door, if not to help then just for the voyeuristic thrill, and looking out through their peepholes see he and Joel standing there, hands in pockets, nervous feet dancing as if they needed to find a bathroom?

The second scream was cut short by a crash.

Shit, Curtis thought.

Maybe the other residents—if there were any—wouldn't say anything to the police. People didn't want to be involved, especially people who lived in run-down project apartment buildings where the doors were identified not with molded resin numbers but rather a difference in the paint where those letters had once been. But maybe a cop would wave a few dollars in the face of some sad heroin addict and say, *"This money'll keep you straight for a month; all I need is a description."* Hanging out in the hallway, he decided, was a bad idea. He rushed into the apartment.

Stumbling over a tweed cushion from the overturned sofa, Curtis reached back and pulled Joel into the room. Stan had Mrs. Woldroff by the throat, knife blade flat against her face, whipping her into the air and crashing against the wall. She flailed, arms and legs blurring, as he plowed her head into the wall. Drywall broke under her skull, dusting the air with white particles. Mrs. Woldfroff screamed. Stan drove her headfirst into the wall a second time, crushing her nose.

She screamed again. On the third blow, her arm and legs fell lax and her head rolled on her shoulders, wild hair sprinkled with drywall.

Huffing, Stan dropped her to the floor. "Should've brought a stud finder, would've saved time." Pointing with the knife, Stan called out to Joel. "Kid, when your teacher was in the classroom, what did you want to do to her?"

Joel crossed his arms. "Do? I dunno what you—"

"Do, yeah, do," Stan said, dropping down over Mrs. Woldroff. With a quick flick of his wrist, the knife snipped off the top button of her blouse. "What were you daydreaming about doing to her in that classroom? Don't be shy. We've all been there, teased by women we can't have. But that's it, Joel, that's *exactly* it: you can have her. She can't stop you anymore. You can do anything you want to her."

"I—" Joel stammered, "—I don't—"

"DAMN IT, BOY!" Stan roared. "WHAT DID YOU WANT? To strip her naked? Feel her up? Did you want to bend her over her desk and FUCK HER? Or maybe..."

Stan snatched Joel's collar and pulled him down. Now kneeling over the prostitute, he slid the knife into Joel's quivering hand. "Or maybe you wanted to hurt her, maybe just a little bit, a tiny little cut—"

Curtis, standing over them, glanced over his shoulder to the doorway. If someone had been standing there, a neighbor perhaps, or a cop with service pistol drawn, he wasn't sure whether he would have felt a stab of panic or wave of relief. But the question was moot and the hall was empty.

Stan guided Joel's hand, dragging the blade between Mrs. Waldroff's breasts, slicing off buttons, until the front clasp of her red bra was exposed.

Stan leaned in. His lips parted only millimeters from Joel's ear. As the blade of the knife slid under the bottom prong of the bra's dual latch, he whispered, "Take what you want from her. Just. Take. It."

A tear ran down Joel's face.

"Joel, don't," Curtis said, louder and firmer than he would have expected possible. Joel and Stan's heads shot up, two sets of eyes staring at him intensely, one pleading for help, the other glowering with rage.

"Ignore him. He's a pussy. Cut her."

"—I—"

"Cut her."

"Don't."

Stan's hand tightened over Joel's. The knife blade twisted and the bottom half of the bra came undone. "Look at her. Look at her flesh. You want her. So *do* her."

The woman woke, shuddering, her lips trembling, a staccato rhythm of tiny gasps escaping from her open mouth. She stared down at the knife between her breasts and froze. Her glossy eyes widened. Her pupils expanded. "Pl—uuhh—llee—zzeeee—"

Her word broke the spell, vanishing any illusion of Mrs. Woldroff and replacing her with a desperate woman already too accustomed to the vulgarities of a cruel world, now staring at the razor edge of a hunting knife hovering over her like a medieval pendulum. Her expression was stark and heart wrenching: a frightened pet in the veterinarian's office too aware of what the needle meant.

"Joel," Curtis whispered.

"—lleee—zzeeee—"

Joel's face changed—not his expression, his face itself, as if he'd shed the scales of childhood like a dried snake skin and revealed the adult beneath. Watching the transformation, Stan's eyes narrowed to slits and he leaned into Joel's ear and growled, "Do her now or I will."

Curtis took a step forward. Stan's head whipped around,

his eyes wild and daring, the corners of his mouth turned up in the cruel snarling smile of a rabid dog. "You stay back or I'll do them *both*."

He dropped back on his heels and shuffled to the doorway.

Before Stan could turn, Joel snapped his arm to his chest and swung back, ramming his elbow into the side of Stan's ear. At twelve, Stan had dropped out of karate class after only two months, but from the looks of it, eight weeks had been enough. The force of the blow knocked Stan off balance and he toppled to the threadbare carpet. His hands shot up to his ear and he howled.

Joel leaped to his feet, hunting knife extended down toward the writhing man. He wiped his face free of tears with a sleeve and warned the serial killer, "YOU LEAVE HER ALONE—YOU STAY DOWN—I NEVER WANTED TO HURT HER—I NEVER WANTED ANYTHING FROM HER—ANYTHING—"

But Stan didn't stay on the floor. He rolled onto his knees and straightened up, wobbling, one hand still on his ear. The terrible grin gone, replaced by a slack-jawed expression of surprise and rejection. "WHAT'RE YOU DOING? YOU THINK THERE'S GOING BACK? THERE'S NO GOING BACK—"

Curtis stepped up to his friend's side. "Back down."

Stan shook his head, not answering Curtis' demand but rather conveying his disappointment. "I thought you boys wanted to know the ropes. Wanted to be killers."

Neither of them had an answer to that; they stayed silent.

"It's okay, Joel. You hold on to that knife," Stan said. The smile returned, crossing his face like a zipper coming undone. "I won't need it."

Stan raised his leg, crooked his foot, and brought the full force of his weight down on the prostitute. With the crack of bone and crunch of cartilage, her throat flattened under his boot. Her body exploded into spasms, arms and legs flailing like dying snakes. Mouth gasping, her head dropped to one side as Stan lifted his boot. "That's gonna take some time. It's up to you two, now. Do you let her asphyxiate, or do you show her some mercy and cut her jugular?"

Stan pushed past them, the back of his hand brushing the hunting knife away as he passed Joel, shoulder bumping Curtis. Before disappearing out the door, he dropped Curtis' mom's keys. "I'll walk. I could use some air."

The prostitute continued to thrash on the floor, the sound of her hands and feet rapping against the floor becoming a wild tribal beat. Her uncontrollable tossing reminded Curtis of the only fish he'd ever caught, squirming and flopping on the creek's bank. After a while—a *long* while—the fish had become flaccid and still. But its mouth still moved, slowly opening and closing, almost mechanical, for many more minutes.

"We gotta call an ambulance," Joel said, dropping the knife to his side. He had a look of desperation in his glossy eyes. "It looks bad, really, *really* bad, but maybe they can…"

But even a quick glance—and that was almost all that Curtis could stand—told a different story. Her head was propped too far to one side for the neck ever to be reconstructed on an operating table. The skin hung loosely from the curve of her collarbone to her jaw, as fluid and lazy as a flap of a canvas tent, quivering with each attempt at a breath. Tear streams ran from her eyes, flowing freely down her temples. Before tonight, outside of the Internet and his grandfather's body at his funeral, Curtis had never seen a real dead body, but knew with absolute certainty that if he stood there long enough, he would. There was no saving her.

"We have to go," he said.

Joel shook his head. "We can't just leave her."

"We can't help her. We have to go."

Joel leaned down over her. "I can't leave her...*like this*."

Knowing the answer to the question he was about to ask, he reached down for Joel's collar. "What are you doing?"

In seventh grade, Curtis and Joel's science class dissected Cuban tree frogs. They'd talked about it for weeks before the day came, anticipating all of the key moments with religious glee: slicing open the amphibian's belly, rooting inside its body cavity, removing organs and pinning them to a chart. If ever there was a class they actually looked forward to attending, this was it.

But when the dissection class came, things changed. They hadn't realized that they would be asked to euthanize the frog first. Wearing a pair of thick yellow gloves, Curtis, the leader, found he could not apply the benzocaine ointment to the frog's back. He kept imagining the sensations the frog must feel: the growing numbness and disorientation, sickness and panic, the shutdown of internal organs. The frog still alive, he removed his gloves.

Joel, the follower, had to finish the project.

He applied the ointment and cut the frog up.

Sitting in the SUV, it was a long time before either of them spoke. It wasn't as if there was nothing to say, in fact exactly the opposite was true. Curtis had a million things he wanted to tell Joel. And all of them seemed to begin with *it's not fair*. But how childish was that? Instead, he sat in the driver's seat and watched Curtis rub the palms of his hands as if the prostitute's blood were still on them; as if it had stained his skin and the bar soap in her bathroom had not been able to wash it away.

Curtis stopped at their usual haunt, not wanting to head home without talking first. It was more than just the need to get their stories straight should the police come around with questions; he suspected it was a matter of survival for their friendship.

Through the windshield, Curtis watched as a trio of teenage girls in miniskirts and midriff tops pranced out of the convenience store doors with oversized fountain drinks and candy bars in their hands, laughing and jabbering away. On any other night, he would have picked out his favorite, compared notes with Joel, and discussed what he wanted to do with the girls. Actually, Curtis realized, Joel never really added much to those conversations beyond *yeah, dude* and *oh, man.*

There would be no staring at girls tonight. Curtis turned his attention fully to Joel. "You okay?"

"No." Barely a whisper, maybe not even meant to be heard at all, Joel stopped rubbing his hands and curled them into fists. "I'm not sure I'll ever be okay again."

Curtis reached over to drop a hand on his best friend's shoulder, but Joel ducked away. That was strange. Normally, Joel would put a hand over his and squeeze for a quick moment, nothing strange, just a confirmation of their friendship. But tonight he slinked away. "We didn't..."

"We didn't WHAT?" Joel said, turning to fully face him. "We didn't kill her? Would she be alive today if we didn't ask that psychotic asshole to show us the goddamn ropes? No, Curt, we killed her all right, we did that. Maybe you can lie to yourself, but I can't. I slit her throat, man, cut her from ear to ear. And you know what? It's what we came out here tonight to do, isn't it? So how are we innocent? Tell me that: how are we not murderers?"

"I—" Curtis protested, but there was nothing more to the defense, just that one word. Finally, when enough time passed and the empty silence became too heavy on his chest, he finished, "I'm sorry."

"Just drive me home."

He did.

They stopped only once more, at a traffic light in the center of town. As they waited, a beaten-up convertible pulled up in the lane beside them. Music blared from the car speakers, too loud for any instrument to stand out; it was just noise. The three boys in the car sneered at them. The driver extended a middle finger and yelled, "Nice hybrid, fags—"

Curtis stared at the light and pretended not to hear them. Joel closed his eyes and sunk into the passenger seat. When the light turned green, Curtis hesitated before stepping on the gas pedal, allowing the convertible to get out in front of them. Curtis bit his bottom lip. "They're just assholes."

"What does that make us?" Joel said without opening his eyes.

He dropped Joel off at his house and they parted with a single sad nod. A nod between best friends could mean many things: *hey, how are you?, let's get outta here, we're cool, right?*

This nod meant nothing.

Curtis cried on his way home. Everything had changed. He wondered if he and Joel would even remain friends. Had the night made it impossible? Could they ever be in the same room without thinking of the prostitute's last breath, a raspy exhale that sounded like an accusation?

Home. Even the sight of it felt unreal, as if his normal life could no longer exist, as if the house continued to stand in opposition to some law of physics that demanded his life before tonight erased in its entirety.

Pulling into the driveway, a buzzing caught his ears and directed his eyes to the dashboard. His cell phone's display blinked off and the body stopped vibrating. Fetching the phone, he saw that he had a missed call. Had the engine been too loud, or had his mind simply been too busy to notice? It didn't matter. He stepped out of the car and pressed REDIAL.

It rang.

The front door was unlocked. Stepping through, he listened for his mom with his free ear. The television chattered in the living room. He was confident he could sneak past without her hearing him from the couch. He didn't feel up to mother-son chit-chat.

The phone rang a sixth time. Then Joel's voicemail picked up. Curtis hung up. The MESSAGE icon blinked on. He dialed out.

"You have one new message," an electronic voice, ostensibly feminine, informed him. "To hear your message, please press—"

He pressed the button.

"First unheard message:"

Creeping up the stairs, Curtis stripped out of his T-shirt as he headed to his bedroom. He didn't think he'd gotten any blood on it, but couldn't be sure. The entire night was already becoming blurry in his memory.

Joel's voice came on, loud and panicked. "CURT, MAN, DON'T GO HOME. YOU CAN'T GO HOME. HE PLAYED US, MAN. THEY— JESUS, MAN, MY PARENTS— DON'T STOP TO CALL ME BACK, JUST GO—GET AWAY— GET—"

A hand grabbed his arm as he reached the landing, jerking him to the side. He fought, shoving his assailant, but lost the brief battle when the arms multiplied. Flung against the wall, his vision doubled and the three men pinning him up became six, all wearing flesh-colored stockings over their heads, their features distorted by the fabric. He writhed for a moment, trying to break free, but their grips were too solid. When one wrapped a strong hand over his throat and squeezed, he froze.

And noticed that they were covered in blood.

He knew then his mother was dead.

The cell phone dropped to the floor.

Another man, also wearing a stocking, came out of his bedroom with a rolled copy of Playboy in one hand. He pointed at Curtis' chest with the magazine. "It's funny, we found dirty magazines under your buddy Joel's bed, too. But they had a different slant, if you get what I'm saying."

He could hear Joel's voice, screaming and rambling, from the cell phone's tiny speaker at his feet. Then Joel's voice cut out. He instantly felt alone.

The man in the stocking snickered. "What did you think, Curtis? Who did you think you were contacting on the message board? Just a bunch of guys that talk about killing because we're bored? We're not bored. We're monsters. I don't think you knew what a monster was before tonight. You didn't even mask your IP address."

The bottom of his stomach fell out. Gravity doubled.

"It was beautiful. You were like an offering from the gods, dressed out on a Thanksgiving serving platter for us. We're in the business of stalking. You made it *so* easy."

A hunting knife clicked open.

"You know, Curtis, you really sort of remind me of my son."

"Pluh—leee—eeeezz—"

"Do you have any idea how much that kid has cost me in college tuition? It's obscene. I have to hold down two jobs. I get so tired that even my...hobby...gets to feel like work sometimes. But I think this time'll be okay. You know why, Curtis? Because it helps if you can imagine someone you know."

\<Giving the Finger\>
Keith Gouveia

"Which hand would you rather I take from?" Mike asked, and Peter was moved by the compassion.

With the forum infiltrators dealt with, there were no reasons to delay the victory ceremony any longer. The thought of killing Mike before he had the chance to chop off one of his digits was still prominent in Peter's mind, but logic told him he could manage far better with one less pinky than he could without Mike.

"The left," he finally answered, "but I'm going to need alcohol first. Lots of alcohol."

The two shared a smile before leaving the basement.

While Mike sterilized the kitchen table and his butcher knife, Peter set out gauze then knocked back a half bottle of scotch. With his body warm, tongue numb, and his mind sufficiently enveloped in an alcoholic fog he sat down at the table and placed his left hand down, pinky finger stretched outward from his other fingers.

"Never done this to a live person before." Mike half smiled as he placed one hand down on the table and hovered the large blade over Peter's helpless digit. "Ready?"

"As I'll ever be…" Peter's slurred words turned into a hiccup.

"Better try to keep still," Mike said, lining up the blade's edge with the base of Peter's knuckle. "I wouldn't want to take more than one."

"O-kay."

"On three. One...two...!"

"Jesus all mighty!" Blood squirted, decorating the table in a crimson flurry. Peter's eyes watered instantly as the pain sobered him and there Mike was, standing dumbfounded as his severed pinky flexed its final movement.

"Mike!"

"Right. Sorry," Mike said as he fumbled to pack gauze into Peter's hand. "Apply pressure while I get the blade good and hot."

"Dear God in heaven it hurts."

"I imagine."

"Bullshit you can," Peter argued. "Give me your finger!"

Mike shook his head, his eyes wide with fear of the possible retaliation.

Blood soaked through the gauze and the more pressure Peter applied, the higher the pain spiked. "Hurry up with that."

"I'm doing my best."

"You should have had that ready to go. I'm starting to feel…woozy."

"Don't you dare pass out," Mike said.

"Mike… I'm proud of the man you've become."

"Peter?"

Mike's words were distant, a faint echo to Peter's ears. His vision blurred. The walls around him warped and swayed. The light slowly faded as the shadows stretched across his line of vision.

"Peter, stay with me."

The world fell silent as the darkness consumed him.

Peter slowly awoke to find himself tucked tightly in his bed. His gaze locked on his throbbing hand and he raised it up to get a closer look. The bandages were clean and it was obvious to him, Mike had been taking real good care of him.

The door to his room opened and Mike stepped inside with a bowl of water and a fresh towel draped over his arm.

"You're awake. Good, I was beginning to worry that I needed to call a doctor."

"Be hard explaining that one." Peter smiled.

"Right?" Mike said playfully as he approached the bedside. "Let me take a look at those bandages."

"They're fine. I just checked them."

Mike placed the bowl of water on the night stand and said, "I used to think you were indestructible."

"C'mon... I—"

"Let me finish," Mike interrupted, "I was petrified of you."

"Yeah, and now?"

"Now, I think I respect you."

Peter smiled at Mike's words and his awkward posture.

"Let's never do this again."

"What? But you've got to give me a chance to get even."

"I don't think you've got enough fingers." Mike smiled a toothy grin.

"Ho-Oh! Cocky. We'll just see about that."

meet the members

C.A. Burns resides in the Midwest with her husband where she writes dark fiction and horror. Her short stories appear in several anthologies and she is working on many more terrible tales.

Kevin Cockle...Living in Calgary, Canada, Kevin is a former boxing journalist, frequent contributor to *On Spec* magazine, and occasional screenwriter. With a background in finance, and an education in critical theory, Kevin's work often explores the odd dialectic between economics and the weird.

Lorne Dixon lives and writes off an exit of I-78 in residential New Jersey. He grew up on a diet of yellow-spined paperbacks, black-and-white monster movies, and the thunder-lizard backbeat of rock-n-roll. His novels *Snarl* and *The Lifeless* are available from Coscom Entertainment.

Keith Gouveia is a Mechanical Engineer who writes fiction in his spare time. His latest releases, *Animal Behavior and Other Tales of Lycanthropy* and *The Black Cat and the Ghoul* have been well received and come highly recommended. Also, look for *The Goblin Princess*, his Young Adult Fantasy novel re-released by The Library of Fantasy, an imprint of The Library of the Living Dead.

Giovanna Lagana is an award-winning freelance author and editor, who loves to work with authors on their stories as well as to create her own. In both instances, she gets to escape reality and travel into worlds of fiction to meet the most interesting and memorable characters.

Some of her short stories and poems have been featured in magazines like *Tales of the Talisman*, *Short-Story.Me*, *Static Movement*, and *Fear and Trembling Magazine*, etc.

To learn more about her and her writings, please check out her website at *giovannalagana.com* .

Mark Onspaugh is a California native who was raised on a steady diet of horror, science fiction and DC Comics. He wrote *Kill Katie Malone* and co-wrote the cult hit *Flight of the Living Dead*. He is an active member of The Horror Writers Association (HWA) and the International Thriller Writers (ITW). He has sold stories to numerous anthologies, including *Fallen from Northern Frights*, Parsec's *Triangulation: End of the Rainbow* and *Triangulation: Dark Glass*, Hadley-Rille's *Footprints*, Eposic's *The Book of Exodi*, Northern Frights' *OZ: Shadows of the Emerald City* and *The World is Dead* from Permuted Press. His essay *"Evilution: A Short History of Monsters from Black & White to Blood Red"* will appear in Dark Scribe Press' *Butcher Knives and Body Counts: Essays on the Formula, Frights and Fun of the Slasher Film*.

Gerald S. Parker was born in New Jersey but moved to Pennsylvania at an early age. Corrupted by Star Trek and Marvel Comics, he began writing. Currently, thanks to the economy, he's pursuing this career full-time. Parker has published numerous stories and one full-length novel in other genres, under other names. "*Hackwork*" is his first foray into horror/suspense, but is unlikely to be the last. He lives in Lancaster County, Pennsylvania.

In addition to being a member of the SFWA, IAMTW, and SFPA, **Marsheila (Marcy) Rockwell** has authored three novels for Wizards of the Coast, two of which tie into the popular MMORPG, Dungeons & Dragons Online (Skein of Shadows, 2012 and The Shard Axe, 2011), and one of which ties into the fantasy noir Eberron setting (Legacy of Wolves, 2007). She also has a series of Arabian-flavored female-centric sword & sorcery stories out from Musa Publishing, *Tales of Sand and Sorcery*. On the poetry side, she has had multiple Rhysling nominations and currently serves as an editor for the ezine *Mindflights*. She lives in Arizona in the shadow of an improbably green mountain with her Naval officer husband, their three sons, the requisite black lab, and far too many books. A (fairly) current list of her publication credits can be found at *marsheilarockwell.com* .

No matter how **Mr. Seate** starts a story, it inevitably turns to the macabre. It may be told with hard core realism or erotic humor, but it gets his pulse racing enough to pull his corpse from the grave to write something new. He is especially keen on stories that transcend genre pigeonholing. His stories and memoirs appear in numerous magazines, newspapers, anthologies and webzines. You will find many of his works at *troyseateauthor.webs.com*. J. T. currently reposes in Golden, CO.

CPSIA information can be obtained at www.ICGtesting.com
Printed in the USA
LVOW080849031212

309774LV00001B/1/P